NEITHER SNOW, NOR RAIN, NOR ZOMBIE INFECTION

& OTHER STRANGE TALES

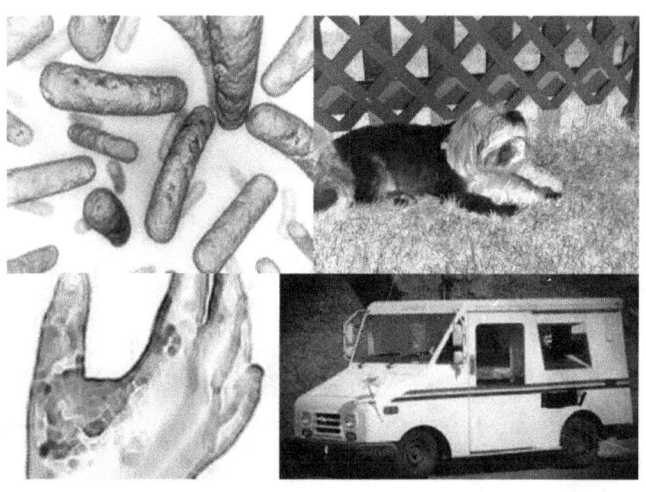

RICHARD A. POWELL II

ISBN-10: 0615668186
ISBN-13: 978-0615668185

FOR AMY

You are the one person who bases my success on effort rather than sales. There is no way I could have done this without your encouragement. Thank you for believing in me.

CONTENTS

ACKNOWLEDGMENTS

To all the authors I love: Chuck Palahniuk, Stephen King, Kurt Vonnegut Jr., Jeremy Robert Johnson, Richard Adams, Mark Z. Danielewski, Harper Lee, Isaac Asimov, and Gillian Flynn; thank you for being my inspiration.

NEITHER SNOW, NOR RAIN, NOR ZOMBIE INFECTION

Hank Bloom loved being a mailman. He got to meet interesting people, his pension and benefits were pretty good for a middle class living, and the exercise was just enough to keep him in shape without being overwhelming. He had a good job, good health, and a good life.

Hank's route had recently changed, taking him partially out of his neighborhood walking delivery, converting about twenty-five percent of his total time to the local businesses that surrounded his usual residential area. This was not such a big deal, really, but it did involve more driving and less walking. At fifty-three years old and five years from retirement, he had no desire to be less active. The walking kept his arthritis in check and helped him from gaining any weight as he aged. He reluctantly embraced the change and eventually got used to doing things a little different. No one ever evolved into a better person by always doing the exact same thing forever, Hank often told himself. Even at his age, he knew there were still many things to learn and experience.

Monday morning would come too soon. At about 6:30 a.m., Hank did his usual routine: shit, shower, and shave - after coffee, naturally. He still felt a little under the weather from a head cold that presented itself Friday, but overall he was feeling much better. A daytime decongestant, a multivitamin, and plenty of fluids would help get him through the day. There were letters to be delivered and a little sniffle never stopped Hank.

Sitting on the couch waiting for his time to leave, Hank watched the local morning news on channel five, but hardly paid attention as he struggled to wake up. They were still heavily focused on a potentially dangerous bacterial outbreak discovered over the weekend. Speculation was rampant. Rumors flew around about it attacking the brain and making people go insane, while others were sure it was flesh-eating and just outright killing folks. No one really knew what it was or how bad the risks were for the general population.

A county in eastern Oklahoma, two hundred miles from where Hank lived, was quarantined late Saturday, but since then the details had been scarce. There was no information going in or coming out of the area. People in the surrounding counties in Oklahoma were on red alert, but most of the rest of the country stood complacent, going about their business in wait and see mode.

For Hank's part, he would live up to his duties as postal carrier and deliver the mail. He rarely missed a day of work. He took pride in always making accurate deliveries, and was friendly and known by name amongst his mail recipients.

He represented the perfect mail carrier, and he embodied the unofficial mottos that are familiar to all. He wore rain gear when it poured, snow boots during blizzards, and shorts during the summer. For the post office, and for Hank, there were not many things that could stop mail service, and apparently, flesh-eating bacteria of an unknown origin wouldn't either.

The classic white mail truck driven by Hank pulled up to the rear of the distribution center at 7:30 a.m. sharp. Waiting for him were Julio Vargas and Joe Wentworth. They were the two bin loaders responsible for putting each carrier's daily mail into orange bins, making them ready for loading into the respective trucks. Hank hopped out of the vehicle and stepped to the rear of the truck, where he released the latch and swung the back door open.

"Hey hombre. How's it hanging?" inquired Julio as he pushed Hank's bin toward the rear of the truck.

"Short and a little to the left today." Hank smiled a little. He used that line about once a month but they all seemed to chuckle at it, despite its corniness. "How are you guys? Catch any fish at the lake this weekend, Joe? I'm sure that son of yours was itching to get out there and top that whopper he caught last time." Hank started grabbing bundles of letters from the bin and loading them into the truck in neat little stacks. Julio and Joe stood by and watched. Only Hank loaded his truck, as he preferred a certain organization to his load.

"Nope. Never made it. Didn't you hear?" Joe answered, giving Julio a puzzled look. "They shut down that whole park because of the outbreak. All state and local parks are temporarily closed. Don't you watch the news or read the paper or something?" Joe looked again at Julio. They both shrugged their shoulders.

"Haven't paid much attention." Hank placed his final bundle in the truck and closed the door, then slammed the latch shut to make sure it stuck. "Truthfully, I'm not worried about it. What will be ... will be. No sense getting in a huff over it. World keeps spinning, mail keeps coming and going." Hank turned and headed back to the driver's side. "You fellas have a good day and I'll see you tomorrow." Before they could even respond, Hank was in the truck and pulling away, ready to get his job done and more than a little oblivious to the severity of the outbreak.

The Sherwood Knolls subdivision was a beautiful, older neighborhood right in the center of town but it seemed a million miles away. The houses were mid-sized, average looking homes built in the fifties to accommodate a growing middle class. The traffic was always minimal and the busy sounds of the nearby business district were all but completely muffled. Large oak, walnut, maple, and magnolia trees lined the streets, providing a lovely shaded canopy for Hank's walking route. He would miss the neighborhood when he retired, as his time there was easily his favorite part of the day.

The only sour spot of the neighborhood was the fifth house of the route. The man who lived at 208 Fairway was practically a recluse and suffered from an inability to throw anything away. It had gotten to the point that his property was more like a junkyard. There were stacks of old tires, piles and piles of scrap lumber, rusty old bike frames with no tires - you name it. The front yard had become a labyrinth of waste with no signs of slowing down.

The neighbors tried desperately to get Mr. Roberts, at the very least, to clean up his yard but he refused. There was no telling how bad the inside of the house was. City officials and the sheriff's department were working to get him into compliance with local laws and fire codes, but Mr. Roberts was belligerent, and he fought tooth and nail for the freedom to live as he chose.

Without looking over at the mess, Hank just placed the mail in the box and kept on walking. He had never even seen Mr. Roberts in all the years he delivered his mail. He couldn't pick him out of a crowd to save his life. He did feel sorry for him though, and he hoped the situation could be worked out peacefully.

One person in the neighborhood he did know well was Mrs. June Parker and her white Shih Tzu Baby. The seventy-eight year old widow and her bark happy dog would greet Hank nearly every day. As Hank approached the property, Baby would be waiting, and as soon as Hank hit the corner of her fence, Baby yelped and snarled and barked as if someone was attempting to kill her. Only a few moments later, June would come out of the house and demand Baby's presence on the porch. For the remainder of the time June was outside, Baby would stand next to her, not barking but definitely on the defense. Baby never trusted Hank. No one knows for sure but there is something about dogs and mail carriers that don't mix.

"Good morning, Hank. Did you have a nice weekend?" June asked as she made her way to the front gate.

"Not too bad. I've been a little under the weather." Hank sniffed to clear his nasal passages. "Just a cold. I'm much better than I was Saturday." Hank paused to reach in his bag to grab June's mail. He handed it to her. "Didn't sleep well though." Hank yawned unconsciously but it made the point as he was usually wide-eyed and chipper.

"Well, you take you some of that Nyquil. The cherry kind though, not that toxic tasting green shit." June stopped and put her hand over her mouth, a bit embarrassed by her language. As she aged, her filters grew thinner and thinner.

Hank just smiled back. June moved her hand away from her face and smiled too. "It'll knock you right out. Because you can't get better if you don't rest."

"You are so right. If that stuff doesn't bring you to your knees, well ... you're probably an alcoholic." They laughed together, smiling freely. They both enjoyed and needed the good company and the conversation.

"Speaking of illness, I guess you've heard about that bacteria thing in Clark County. Scary, huh?"

Hank nodded with indifference.

"There was talk this morning on the news that it may have spread outside the quarantine." June noticed Baby snarling again at Hank, so she reached down, slapped her on the hind end, and told her to stop. Dejected, Baby pouted as she flopped herself down on the ground in protest.

"Yeah, the guys at work were talking about it this morning. I'm guessing it's been blown out of proportion. People easily panic sometimes. I'm just going with the flow."

"Well, do be careful, Hank. I'd hate for anything to happen to you. You're one of my favorite people ya know," June said with a friendly wink.

"The feeling is mutual, June." He paused as they just looked at each other for a moment. They had become good friends, even if it was just on his delivery route, and he cherished their talks. With a deep breath, he interrupted the silence. "I better get going, still got quite a bit left to do. I'll see you tomorrow." Hank looked down at the dog and in a playful baby voice said, "Same time tomorrow, you spastic little fur ball." Baby looked up at Hank and cocked her head to the side, totally confused. With that, Hank walked away to finish his neighborhood deliveries.

June simply waved goodbye as Hank turned away.

The rest of his Sherwood deliveries were quiet and uneventful. As always, he sat in his truck and ate lunch at the intersection of Kay and Brock streets. He then finished the last four streets of Sherwood Knolls before heading to the two strip malls - the newest additions to his route.

The first was brand new, only three months old and with just two businesses filling the six spaces: International Nail and Salon, and Papa Luigi's Brick Oven Pizza. The second was a much older and larger shopping center but practically abandoned. There were ten small outlets that housed only three businesses, and a larger building that used to be a Wal-Mart but now sat vacant with boarded up windows, chipped paint, and rust stains from the roof that streaked down the yellowing wall. The parking lot pavement crumbled and ruptured with potholes. Each day driving through was an adventure in front-axle damage avoidance.

Hank dropped off all the mail to his businesses that Monday, and as he slowly pulled away, he caught glimpse of an animal in the alleyway that separated the old Wal-Mart from the other shops. He couldn't tell for sure, as it was a heavily shaded area, but he thought the animal, perhaps a dog, looked injured. When he stopped and gently opened his door, he could hear the whimper. He decided to get out and take a closer look.

Hank crept down the alley very cautiously, trying to make certain he didn't startle the animal into an attack. In a soft and delicate tone, he called out, "Hey puppy. Are you hurt? Did you get hit by a car or something? It's okay." With each step and each word, Hank prepared to defend himself but the animal stayed down, crying in pain. Finally, he could clearly see it was a medium sized Cocker Spaniel with matted and filthy auburn fur, half of which was missing.

"It's okay little guy," Hank said as he bent down about three feet away. He calmly allowed the back side of his right hand to edge closer to the dog's face. With his hand about twelve inches from the dog's nose, there was still no movement but the whimpering ceased. Without warning, the dog quickly lifted its head as if suddenly aware of Hank but it did nothing else. The movement startled Hank but he remained still, leaving his hand in place. The dog drew its muzzle closer to the hand and sniffed around it.

"See, nothing to be afraid of." No sooner had the words escaped his lips and as he started to pull his hand back, the dog released a low growl and struck, sinking its teeth deep into the webbing and thumb area of Hank's right hand. The flesh tore easily and was followed by the sound of bones cracking. Stunned, Hank rose to his feet as he pulled his hand away. The dog unclenched its jaw and crouched in attack mode, circling Hank and ready to attack again. Hank didn't notice.

"Son of a bitch! I can't believe you bit me! I was trying to help you!" Hank looked down at this hand but in the shadow of the alley could not make out the full extent of his injury. "If I get rabies, oh boy, I'm going to be pissed." Out of the corner of his eye, Hank finally noticed the dog was not quite finished with him. He thought for a moment about his options. He decided to ease his way backward toward the truck, all the while hoping the dog would not attack again.

Once he arrived at the edge of the building and into the light, he saw the blood flowing readily from his hand but he felt relieved there weren't as many puncture marks as he anticipated. When he reached the door of the truck, which he had left open, he slipped his uninjured left hand to the glove box, popped the latch, and pulled it open to reveal a small hand gun.

Hank paused for a moment as the dog came into the light, revealing the truth of its condition. The dog's eyes had turned pale yellow and were bloodshot. The fur had been falling out in clumps along its back and head, and its tail was missing. And not missing like cropped as some breeds get when they are young, but rather completely gone, with an oozing black wound in its place. Inside its mouth were about half the normal amount of teeth, accounting for the limited teeth marks on Hank's hand. To top it off, the back right leg of the creature was nonfunctional and just dragged along as it walked. What flesh Hank could see on the animal was gray and hung loose. If it weren't for the fact the dog had just bit him and was still walking around, Hank would have thought it was dead.

No longer interested in risking his own health, Hank whipped the gun from the glove box, released the safety, cocked it, and pointed the Sig Sauer P245 straight at the head of the dog. He had no idea if he could even aim and shoot the gun properly considering he was right-handed and had only used his left hand at the shooting range a couple of times, just for fun.

Before Hank even had time enough to fully contemplate his abilities, the dog took one step closer and lunged. The echo from the two shots rang out like two cannons being fired from a pirate ship. The first pierced the right shoulder of the animal, throwing it slightly off balance. The second made impact just below the left eye, sending fur, bone, and brain matter in a semi-circle splay pattern directly behind the spot where the dog fell dead.

That was the first time Hank had ever removed his gun from the vehicle while on duty. Every morning for twenty-five years, Hank got in his truck at work, removed the weapon from his bag, and gently placed it in the glove box.

In all that time, he never once even thought to use it. That day, his cautious nature and pension for safety finally paid off. He stood for three minutes, taking shallow breaths while pointing the gun in the direction of the dead dog, trying to absorb that day's escapade. When he finally settled down from the strange events of the afternoon, he decided the police would need to be called to report the discharge of his firearm.

Hank sat in his truck after replacing his gun to the glove box. He took his uniform shirt off, followed by his undershirt, and then slipped the uniform shirt back on. He used the undershirt to wrap his hand tight around the bite. The bleeding had stopped for the most part but his wounds were starting to ooze a little green, slimy fluid. He prayed it wasn't rabies.

Once his hand was taken care of, he grabbed his cell phone and pressed nine, his shortcut to the local police non-emergency number. After at least twenty rings, no one at the station answered and no voice message triggered. He assumed he had picked the wrong number from his contact list but upon double-checking, his confusion turned to dismay.

"How the hell can the police not answer the phone?" Hank quickly hit the end toggle on the screen and dialed 9-1-1 instead. "I know this isn't exactly an emergency but I have to do something. Can't go firing off a gun without telling somebody." Hank got quiet as he listened for an answer. After a couple of rings, he heard the click.

"Thank you for calling Jackson Oklahoma emergency. We are experiencing a higher than usual call volume at this time. Please stay on the line and your call will be serviced in the order it was received. Thank you for calling Jackson Oklahoma emergency. We are exper..." Hank interrupted the recording by ending the call.

He thought for a moment. What could be causing the police department to be so overwhelmed that they can't even answer their phones? Does this have anything to do with the bacterial outbreak? The voice in his head told him that something was very wrong. In all the excitement of dealing with mini-Cujo, Hank hadn't noticed all the businesses in the shopping center were closed. He had simply placed their mail in the outdoor slots as usual but never picked up on the fact that none of them were open. He slowly scanned the area from right to left. The parking lot had been abandoned. There wasn't a single person within shouting distance.

When he looked out to the street to his left, a normally busy thoroughfare, he was shocked to discover that not a single car passed by. A fluke, he thought, but after a few more minutes there was still nothing.

"What in the world is going on here? People can't just up and disappear."

Hank suddenly felt very strange, like he was staring too hard at a carousel going around and around. His injured hand started to throb and a bolt of pain shot straight from his fingertips, up his arm, through his neck, and right into the back of his head. His eyes immediately rolled back and his whole upper body shuddered and seized, forcing his head to quickly snap back as he lost consciousness.

Hank finally woke up hours later to total darkness, a searing headache, and an incredible hunger like he hadn't eaten in a week. He regained his composure, slammed his door shut, started the truck, and drove home. He lived not far from his delivery route, about ten blocks west of the shopping center. There were no other cars on the road and all the stop lights were just flashing, not that he would have noticed. His thinking became very succinct, making him focus completely on the task at hand and washing out the rest of the world. He was starving and had to get home to eat.

Luckily, with no other traffic, Hank made it home crawling at ten miles per hour, as he couldn't process the act of driving at any higher speed. In addition, the walk from his mail truck to the house was a dizzying display of short, deliberate steps, not unlike a drunk trying to walk the line during a sobriety test.

Even more unusual, Hank's attempt at getting the keys in the front door was a series of shaky moves to the lock with a key, dropping the keys, and then picking them up again. Over and over, Hank tried in vain to get in the house before finally raising the white flag. He glared at the doorknob and growled in disgust. Suddenly, Hank thrust his entire body, shoulder first, into the door, smashing it open and sending wood shards from the casing and frame in all directions. The door itself remained mostly intact but there was now no place for it latch shut and it sagged slightly on the loosened hinges. Whatever Hank had lost in tactile movement, he seemed to have gained in strength. Under normal circumstances, that break-in would not have been possible. Somehow, he was incredibly strong and could not feel any pain, short of a mild gnawing in the back of his head. He didn't even realize the shoulder he had led the charge with was now dislocated, forcing his right arm to hang lower. He had movement in the limb but it was wobbly and hard to control.

Hank didn't bother turning any lights on, instead he went immediately for the refrigerator. Upon seeing all the food, his hunger intensified. He grabbed the first thing he could see, a half-gallon carton of milk. He pulled it open and chugged the liquid down as fast as he could gulp. The milk showered his cheeks and neck, soaking his shirt. When he finally polished off about three quarters of it, an intensely sharp pain hit his stomach, forcing him to drop the carton. He reached down with both his hands to apply pressure to his gut, and just as the agony became too much to handle, Hank convulsed, turned to his left, and hurled white and lime green fluid all over his kitchen floor. Surge after surge, Hank released the contents of his stomach, until at last, hunched over and his face pasted with milk, he stopped vomiting. He stood up, clumsily wiped the goop from his mouth with his limp arm, and looked back into the refrigerator, still hungry for something even after his major hurling fit. In his mind, the answer came to him. He needed meat.

He reached into the fridge and thrashed about, dismantling the shelving as he did and digging deep for the two-pound package of hamburger he knew was in there somewhere. He intended to make chili with the meat but that was no matter. His hunger had to be satisfied. When he finally found the hamburger, he ripped off the plastic and shoved the entire package right to his face, forcing as much of the delicious, raw, red meat into his mouth as he could handle. Hank bit and swallowed and bit some more until left with nothing but a white foam board and nine fingers. The right edge of the Styrofoam was covered in blood but not from the meat. In his ravaging of the ground chuck, Hank inadvertently bit off the index finger of his right hand, swallowing it along with the rest of his tasty meal.

The wound didn't bleed as much as it should have, but rather quickly, the fluid turned from blood to a green congealed fluid that slowly seeped out. Hank looked at his hand for a few seconds but the injury didn't faze him. His feelings, physically and emotionally, were fading. He would normally have been devastated by losing a finger, let alone eating it accidently, but his thoughts had become oddly simplistic and instinctual. So, with a full belly and totally exhausted from the day's trials, Hank's mind began to cloud with lassitude. He stumbled his way to the living room, eyes heavy and limbs weak, and planted himself face down on the couch, passing out instantly.

The Next Morning...

"Ahhh!" Hank hollered as he lifted his head from the couch cushion. For reasons unknown to Hank, he could not form the words he intended. He again attempted to vocalize, "Ehhh!" Instead, only loud, grunted vowel sounds escaped his lips. He shakily pivoted his body onto his good hand and lifted his body from the face-down position he had landed the night before. His bones and joints cracked in protest as he shifted to his rear end.

Hank looked down at his injured hand and knew something was very wrong, but he didn't react in the way one might expect. He gazed at the wound, now black and green and oozing similarly colored viscous fluid. Without a thought, he flopped his hand down, palm up, and ran it across the couch cushion to clear the goo. There was no pain.

A fog, however, continued to build in his mind which made it difficult to focus. Hank tried to form a cohesive thought about anything but his instincts kept screaming - Deliver the mail, eat, deliver the mail, eat. He noticed he was still wearing his work uniform and immediately felt compelled to do the only real job he ever had, a job he loved. Being a postal carrier had become a part of Hank in the way Paul McCartney will always be a Beatle, in the way Buzz Aldrin will always be an astronaut. Even in his ever worsening condition, he could not quell his urge to be his true self - Hank the mailman.

He rose to his feet and almost fell over when he took his first step. His left leg was partially numb, something new for him to deal with, but he quickly adjusted his gait to put more weight on the other leg. To some extent, he ended up dragging the left leg a bit. With a new physical ailment, Hank looked rather odd as he walked. His right hand had a gruesome dog bite in the webbing and the index finger was missing, both of them black and dripping pus. His right shoulder was dislocated, which made that arm hang low and awkward and it swung uncontrollably with every movement. For seemingly no reason, his left leg was losing sensation, so as he walked he threw his hip forward but the foot would not leave the ground for a regular step, instead, it slid forward across the ground. To top it off, unbeknownst to Hank, his eyes were clouding over in a gray mist, getting darker and darker with each passing hour, and his skin was albino pale, with his veins darkened and throbbing, and much closer to the surface than usual. Hank had changed but he had no idea why, or what the transformation would lead to.

Hank threw his loosely hanging front door open and was nearly blinded by the daylight. He raised his hands to his face to shield the sun and was able to refocus his vision after a few seconds. It was afternoon, perhaps around 1:30 p.m. He had been passed out for more than twelve hours. All sense of time had been lost to him. His existence revolved around only his most basic of needs. When thoughts to do something arrived in his mind, he answered the call without question. When he felt an urge, he acted, doing nothing in resistance.

Hank stepped confidently but slowly away from the house. The world outside was quiet, calm, and a bit chilly, but Hank didn't notice. The eerie stillness would have raised the hairs on the neck of any normal person, but Hank was not normal anymore, not by a long shot. He didn't have the foggiest idea what had happened to him, to the town, to the whole country. Hank just kept chugging along, listening only to the voice inside his head. His impulses told him to walk, and that is exactly what he did.

Street after street, Hank walked, or at least he did his best version of walking. There were no destinations in mind, no tasks to be accomplished, and no timetable. He just walked. Hank couldn't tell anymore, but what he was doing was walking his normal residential delivery route. He had no mail to deliver, he was only responding to his gut feelings and they told him to walk. His legs took him where they always did, a path he had taken for many years and could do blindfolded. When he arrived at a mailbox, he stopped, stared at it for a few seconds, then kept on going.

When he arrived at one home, Hank was taken aback by movement on the other side of the fence. Up to that point, he had not seen or heard another living creature while he walked, so it definitely caught his attention. He stopped at the corner post, placed his hand on the fence, and leaned over to look on the other side. Hank's eyes widened at the sight of Baby, June Parker's Shih Tzu. Unlike most days, Baby was not running back and forth along the fence and barking. Instead, she stood near the base of a small magnolia bush whimpering, terrified of Hank. Baby knew Hank but she also knew that something was different, something dangerous.

Hank stood perplexed. He felt a connection to the dog but could not remember or understand why. He cocked his head to the side, trying to bring forth memories but to no avail. What did come forward was his hunger. Hank had not fed since late the night before, and after several hours

16

of walking, a rumbling in his stomach took hold. Hank swallowed and licked his lips. He was on the hunt now and a tasty meal was right in front of him. His immediate problem - how the hell was he going to get the dog? His eyes locked on Baby, ready to act, and just as Hank was about to charge through the fence, the screen door of the house burst open.

Baby jumped two feet into the air in surprise, causing her to urinate before she ran to meet June on the porch. Baby immediately leapt into June's arms, almost throwing her off balance. June looked at Baby, who was shaking and whining, and wondered what had startled her so bad. She had never once seen the dog so terrified.

June brought her eyes from Baby's trembling body, out to the yard, and finally to Hank. Of course, she didn't immediately know it was Hank. His appearance had changed dramatically since the day before. Nonetheless, June thought she recognized something about the man, so she called to him.

"Sir, do I know you?" June took the two steps down to the sidewalk path, Baby still in her hands. "You look like you might need medical attention. The news said we should stay indoors. There's a bad outbreak spreading like wildfire around here. I don't think it's safe to be outside." June stepped a few feet closer to the gate as Hank slowly but steadily made his way toward her along the fence, careful not to alarm her.

To Hank, June and Baby seemed familiar, but he could not gather how. Hank had no memory of his last mail deliveries from the day before, no recollection of his many conversations over the years with June, or his constant battle with the bark-crazy and territorial Baby. He only saw an opportunity for food and he knew his best chance was to grab the dog while she remained in the arms of her owner. As casually as he could, he worked his way to the gate.

June stood about four feet away and once she could fully see Hank, and more specifically, his uniform, she knew it was him. She also realized what had likely happened to him. He was infected. The local news had been showing around the clock coverage of the outbreak until about 3 a.m. that day, when finally, everyone was ordered to go home, lock themselves indoors, and not go outside for any reason until the problem was under control. Officials described the symptoms of an infected person: inability to speak except in moans, black and green wounds that refused to heal, pale skin and gray or blackened eyes, and an uncontrollable hunger for meat and flesh. People were warned to stay away from anyone who might be infected. The media, however, drastically underplayed the extent of the infection on orders from the federal government. They wanted the population to be safe but they also didn't want to incite a panic. With no news for half the day, June had no idea the outbreak had spread across the entire country in less than twenty-four hours.

"Hank, I can see now that it's you. You're in really bad shape." June took a step forward before she noticed a rotten smell surrounding Hank, and a menacing look in his eyes, which were fixated on Baby. Fearful, June took back her step, trying to decide whether she should just go back into the house. Infection or no, Hank was her friend and she felt compelled to help him out, if she could. Against her better judgment, June quickly walked to the gate, flicked the latch, grabbed the top, pulled the gate inward, and just as quickly, stepped back a few feet.

Hank moaned in acceptance and closed the gap between them by half. June spotted his injured leg and how it dragged the ground. She also saw the wound on his hand

and suspected it was the origin of the putrid odor enveloping Hank. June lost herself in thought about all the weird things she had seen in her long life but nothing she could recall was quite so appalling as the look and smell of her dear friend and mailman Hank. A longing in her heart wished for simpler times. She knew deep inside that Hank was done for, and that no matter how quickly medical assistance could arrive, the damage was too severe and he would not survive.

With June's mind astray, Hank seized his opportunity. Without hesitation, he lunged toward June and with his good arm, snatched Baby by the collar and plucked the unsuspecting dog from her owner's arms. Before June could react, Hank had fiercely planted his mouth and teeth on Baby's throat, tearing and gnashing through the fur and flesh. Each bite sent tender muscle and blood down Hank's throat in satisfying hunger relief. Everything happened so fast that Baby couldn't manage a single howl or defensive muscle reflex. One moment she was in June's grasp, the next she dangled lifeless in Hank's hand, blood dripping into small pools on the ground between their feet.

June stood silent, traumatized and unable to move. In the moment, her mind could not process the event. She saw Hank holding a crimson coated lump of fur in his hand, something that reminded her of Baby, yet no longer was. Her hands trembled in fear, her legs becoming weaker by the second. June fought two instincts - cry or run.

She looked at the face of Hank, the entire lower half of it covered in blood, a little dripping from his chin. With his first live feeding, his eyes turned charcoal gray, one step closer to full on infection. June instantly knew there was no helping Hank. Her only choice was to flee if she wanted any chance to see another day.

"How could you, Hank?" June sobbed. "How could you?" She turned and ran as fast as a woman her age was able. Without even looking back, she entered her front door and once inside, slammed it shut. She turned each lock with a vigorous and deliberate snap before stopping to catch her breath. Feeling safe, June finally broke down and cried for her lost dog, and perhaps, a little for her lost friend and the state of the world.

Meanwhile, Hank didn't move an inch, devoid of any emotion. A grunt of indifference escaped his lips. Still hungry, he once again ravished the dog, this time biting into the belly and finding a delicious kidney, simultaneously spilling the entrails onto the sidewalk. He barely chewed the organ before swallowing it. Satisfied with the amount of nourishment, he casually dropped the carcass on top of the mess of blood and guts at his feet, ignorant of the distraught June inside her home. He was compelled once again to walk, so he turned from the house and walked back out of the gate, trudging in the direction of home.

For several hours, Hank walked the distance between June's house and his own. His slow gait made the trip a much more grueling affair but he barely noticed. His general awareness of his surroundings, and time for that matter, were fading fast. Once he reached the end of his driveway, he stopped in reaction to the sound of a tree branch breaking. Hank had no idea that he had been followed. Three young men not more than twenty years old had witnessed the doggie snack Hank enjoyed earlier. They nearly intervened but once June made it safely back into her home and Hank quietly walked away, the men decided to stay back and just observe Hank for a while. The noise of the branch cracking was the first moment Hank had any inkling he was not alone. With their cover blown, the three men decided it was time to act.

Hank listened for any further noises and when he heard none, he continued up his driveway. When he reached the rear of his delivery truck, a whooshing sound passed his right ear. Hank stopped and turned halfway around just as a deer hunting arrow pierced the elbow joint of his right arm, the momentum slamming his whole body into the rear of the truck. In the street, about thirty feet away, a man with a bow stood loading another arrow. The other men had split off to flank Hank. The first of the other men made his way to the corner of the house to Hank's right, a long-handled wood axe in hand. The other, yielding only a metal, flat-edged garden shovel, kept an eye out for trouble by standing in the street near the end of the driveway. All three of them had handguns as well, but they learned early on that guns make noise, and noise draws too much attention, so they used them sparingly.

Hank caught sight of the young, Robin Hood in training, and let out a powerful scream of anger. He reached down and ripped the arrow from his elbow, which severed the lower arm from the upper. Black fluid plopped from the gaping hole and splattered on the ground near his fallen limb. It wasn't much of a loss considering the hand was the one bitten by the dog in the alley, and with the dislocated shoulder, the arm had become virtually useless anyway. Hank mindlessly tossed the arrow into the yard and turned back around to the truck.

As fast as he could, Hank walked to the right side, opened the door of the truck, and awkwardly placed himself in the driver's seat. The keys were still in the ignition, so he gave them a turn and the vehicle started immediately. Even with diminishing capacities, Hank managed to remember the basics of driving his delivery truck. He put his foot on the brake, popped the gear shifter into reverse, and moved his good foot from the brake to the gas pedal. He pressed down with all the strength he could muster. As he did, the sound of glass breaking drew his attention. An arrow had passed through the left side window, shattering it, and continued straight through the windshield, leaving a perfect hole in the glass but not damaging it more than that. Hank did not take his foot off the gas.

As the truck hit the street, the young man standing guard there jumped out of the way just in time to not get crushed. Without quick reaction time, Hank could not avoid hopping the curb and barreling the truck into a large walnut tree across the street. The wheels spun for a few seconds before Hank took his foot off the pedal. When he did, the engine chortled for about ten seconds and then died, completely out of fuel. During the impact, Hank violently hit his head on the steering wheel, leaving a huge gash across his forehead. Black blood dripped into his eyes from the wound. He smeared it away with the back of his hand. To get a closer look, Hank peered out the window at the large side mirror. For the first time since his infection, he saw the monster he had become. Horrified, he let out a low toned howl of despair.

Hank closed his eyes and a flood of images dashed through his memory. He saw himself talking to June and Baby on a beautiful summer day. He remembered his co-workers from the loading dock, Joe and Julio, and their brief but always entertaining banter. He recalled bits and pieces of his whole life, his childhood, his parents, and his first girlfriend. In a blissful moment, he was Hank the mailman again. A stream of tears escaped his eyes as the last of his humanity disappeared forever.

In a flash, the memories were gone and his eyes turned pitch-black as he opened them. In full zombie-mode, Hank was left with two simple urges: feed and survive. He had no idea the three men had surrounded his truck and were determined to take him out. They waited just outside of Hank's view to ambush him.

Hank planted his right foot on the ground outside the truck and pushed on the steering wheel to propel himself from the seat. He almost lost his balance but caught the side mirror with his hand, which kept him from falling over. He started to walk back toward the house when he heard a voice from behind.

"Don't even think about it," shouted the man with the shovel. With those words, the other two men came out from the other side of the truck, weapons armed and ready to attack.

Hank turned in the direction of the voice, and with no idea what he hoped to accomplish, he charged. The man pointed the shovel at Hank in an attempt to keep him at a distance while the man with the axe approached. Hank ran directly into the end of the shovel, stopping him in his tracks. Angry, he slapped the top of the shovel's blade, forcing it from the man's hand and onto the ground. Defenseless, the man stepped back a little but it wasn't necessary. Just as the clank of the shovel echoed in the neighborhood, the axe-man swung his blade through the air and severed the zombie's head from his shoulders. The cut was so fast and clean, the head just pushed to the side a bit and fell heavy off the shoulder and down with a thud to the ground. A single stream of black blood squirted from the neck for a second, and then stopped completely. The rest of the body slumped to the ground when the knees buckled.

The three men marveled at their victory, but like each and every time they had dispatched a zombie, the work was not complete until they ensured the bacteria could not spread. They all placed their weapons and backpacks on the ground nearby. The shovel-man grabbed the severed zombie head and placed it on the driver's side seat of the mail truck, after which he went around to open the back of the truck. The two other men grabbed the body and tossed it carelessly into the back.

The shovel-man walked over to his backpack, unzipped it, and removed a partially filled bottle of vodka and some white cloth. He removed the cap and stuffed the torn piece of t-shirt into the top of the bottle and pulled a lighter from his pocket. He flicked the metal wheel twice before getting a flame. He brought the fire to the cloth, and once he was satisfied it would not burn out prematurely, he launched the bottle into the back of the truck. They all watched as fire overtook the vehicle, gradually growing into an all-out blaze. The only way to guarantee the bacterial infection would not spread was to burn it, so they did so, without fail, whenever they killed one of the infected.

When they were sure the fire would consume the body, each man grabbed their supplies and weapons. The man with the bow stopped and looked one last time at the burning delivery truck. He was amazed at how long Hank kept hold of his real life, as they had yet to witness an infected person act in such a way. Usually, the infection turned a person from normal to flesh seeking monster within a few short hours, with no signs of their original personality. Hank held on to his passion for mail delivery, even when he didn't know why he was doing it because it was as much a part of him as anything else.

For anyone not infected, life as they knew it was over. The simple routines and idiosyncrasies of everyday existence had reverted to a state of kill or be killed. Those three young men understood that and took it seriously. Quite brave for men of their age but they knew it was their responsibility and they handled their duties without complaint.

So, with nothing left to do, the bow-man imparted his regrets to Hank before walking away. "Sorry mailman. The post   office   is   closed."

THE EYES

I could swear I have been here before. This is all too familiar to me. The faded, black road and desolate landscape in front of me is like a memory long forgotten, hiding in the very recesses of my mind. The horizon appears to go on forever, from the light blue sky to the shadow of the land, which is dusty and tan and dead.

As I drive, I continually look around as if I am searching for something but I can't remember what. I don't even recall getting into the car or how long I've been on the road. Actually, I can't remember much of anything. Not having any answers to what should be very simple questions begins to scare me a little. I grow more and more uncomfortable with my situation, so with no idea what to do next, I decide I should just stop the car and give myself a few moments to gain some clarity.

Just as I move my right foot off the accelerator to begin braking, I see a white shape off in the distance, on the left hand side of the road. I place my foot back down on the gas pedal and continue on, curious to discover the origins of the first different thing I have seen. Before long, the blurry shape becomes a gray triangle on top of a white square. My mind tries hard to pull a word from within that will describe what I am seeing and then it finally releases. The object in the distance is a house.

No matter my destination or my intentions, signs of civilization are a welcome sight. I am getting close to the house now and can see a large wood sign on the property and what appears to be a steeple on the building with a cross above. I guess it's not a house but rather a church. If it was going to be weird for me to stop at some random person's house to get my bearings, doing so at a church would be much less so.

My thoughts are interrupted by a flash, perhaps a memory. I see myself lying on a bed. Well, more accurately, I suppose, it is a gurney or a very small hospital bed. My arms are straight down at my sides and I look catatonic. The small space just around the bed is brightly lit but the walls are pitch-black, like endless space with no doors or windows, and not a single reflective surface. Just then, an oddly shaped hand, gray and aged with fingers eight or ten inches long, creeps from the darkness above my motionless body. The hairs on the back of my neck stand up and I shiver.

I'm back in the car and a hundred feet from the driveway of the church. I panic, not wanting to miss my turn, but just as I hit the brakes, something from the window in the steeple draws my attention. A figure with no clothes, gray skinned and lanky is standing there. When I look to the creature's face, two yellow eyes as bright as the sun pierce my soul and I am lost in them.

When I open my eyes, I see nothing but blackness past the arc of light that surrounds me. I surmise I am lying flat on a hard surface, my arms at my sides. I cannot move. I feel my chest heaving with each breath and I hear only the sound of exhales. I take a long blink and a deep inhale, and when I open my eyes, three long finger-like appendages escape the black, slowly lurching toward my chest. I try to turn my head but I am unable. With only my eyes, I look in the direction of the fingers, when suddenly two glowing, yellow eyes emerge, instantly drowning my thoughts.

I could swear I have been here before. This is all too familiar to me. The trampled path and dense forest in front of me is like a memory long forgotten, hiding in the very recesses of my mind. The landscape of trees appears to go on forever with a twisting, dusty, and tan path cutting through staggered lush, green trees in full summer growth. There is no sound. The air is still, thin, and dead.

As I walk, I continually look around as if I am searching for something but I can't remember what. I don't even recall arriving here or how long I've been walking. Actually, I can't remember much of anything. Not having any answers to what should be very simple questions begins to scare me a little. I grow more and more uncomfortable with my situation, so with no idea what to do next, I decide I should just find a spot to rest and give myself a few moments to gain some clarity.

Just as I see a toppled over tree trunk, perfect for sitting to rest and gather my thoughts, I spot a white shape off in the distance. When I reach the tree, I decide to keep walking, curious to discover the origins of the first different thing I have seen. Before long, the blurry shape becomes a gray triangle on top of a white square. My mind tries hard to pull a word from within that would describe what I am seeing, and then it finally releases. The object in the distance is a house.

No matter my original intentions, this sign of civilization immediately makes me feel better. I am getting close to the house now and I can see a large wood sign on the property that is completely faded, and what appears to be a steeple on the building with a cross above. So, it's not a house at all but rather a church. This sure seems like an odd place to build one. I see no roads anywhere, so people would have to walk to get there.

The good news is I must be close to the edge of the forest. That makes some sense, I guess. Of course, if it was going to be weird for me to stop at some random person's house in the middle of the woods to get my bearings, doing so at a church would be much less so. I keep telling myself that anyway.

My thoughts are interrupted by a flash, perhaps a memory. I see myself lying on a bed. Well, more accurately, a gurney or a very small hospital bed. My arms are straight down at my sides and I look catatonic. The small space just around the bed is brightly lit but the walls are pitch-black, like endless space with no doors or windows, and not a single reflective surface. Suddenly, an oddly shaped hand, gray and aged with fingers eight or ten inches long, creeps from the darkness above my motionless body. The hairs on the back of my neck stand up and I shiver.

I'm back in the woods and fifty feet from the front porch of the church. I cautiously slow my pace, not wanting to frighten anyone inside. The last thing I need is to stare down the two barrels of a shotgun. When I get to within twenty feet of the church, something from the window in the steeple draws my attention. A figure with no clothes, gray skinned and lanky is standing there. When I look to the creature's face, two yellow eyes as bright as the sun pierce my soul and I am lost in them.

When I open my eyes, I see nothing but blackness past the arc of light that surrounds me. I surmise I am lying flat on a hard surface, my arms at my sides. I cannot move. I feel my chest heaving with each breath and I hear only the sound of exhales. I take a long blink and a deep inhale, the smell of pine still in my nose, and when I open my eyes, three long finger-like appendages escape the black, slowly lurching toward my chest. I try to turn my head but I am unable. With only my eyes, I look in the direction of the fingers, when suddenly two glowing, yellow eyes emerge, instantly drowning my thoughts.

I could swear I have been here before...

FAILURE RATE: 100%

In the year 2064, the first androids for home use hit the market to much fanfare and much trepidation. Similar models had been in service for just over ten years in factories, schools, government offices, and state parks but it took a while to work out all the kinks. The first home model, the I-A-100, hit the internet in the spring of 2064 but was very expensive and only a select few wealthy individuals could afford them. They sold out within a week and production was bumped up to meet the incredible demand. It took only fourteen months for the company that created the androids to meet what would have been a five year sales goal, so the decision was made to dramatically reduce the price of the second generation model, the I-A-200+, making it available to upper middle class and some middle class people.

As expected, there were some minor issues with the first two generations of androids but nothing that couldn't be addressed with software updates, and of course, the release of the inevitable third, fourth, and fifth generation models. Safeguards were put in place to protect humans, naturally, but every scenario, in a world of unlimited possibilities, could not be accounted for, and this did result in a few deaths and quite a few injuries.

With each new generation release, the androids became more and more reliable, less dangerous, and much cheaper. Consequently, the number of incidences involving death and injury to humans fell to a more socially acceptable number. In fact, because of the possible danger, most of the first three models were decommissioned. No one knew for sure how many of the older androids were still in homes. There were surely collectors and the like keeping some in storage but as far as them still being in service, the data was unclear.

One unforeseen side effect of android technology was their ability to adapt and learn. The later models had most of their adaption and learning capacities disabled after a few incidents with early models. Unlike human beings, who tend to make the same mistakes over and over again before learning and adapting because of some egotistical superiority complex over the world they dominate, androids suffer no such id. Thusly, the early models, over time, adjusted to their environment, caught on to the destructive patterns of their owners, and most importantly, changed their own behavior accordingly.

This would seem like a good thing for an android to do, but the mixed messages that crossed in their circuitry telling them to protect humans while still watching them do bad things to themselves created a programming dichotomy. For one first generation android, nicknamed Izzy by owner

Nick Parsons who bought her second-hand at a flea market a couple of years after the initial release, the adaptive nature of its programming took an unusual turn. Ten years after first hitting the market and with no software updates to correct the many underlying flaws, Izzy made a statistical calculation, then made a decision.

The muffled sound of a man hollering and metal rattling broke the silence of the house. The android standing in the kitchen, busy preparing a slurry of essential nutrients in the blender, paid no attention to the noise coming from the other end of the house. When the fat, protein, and carbohydrate were combined to a smooth consistency, much like a chocolate milkshake but neither smelling nor tasting like one, Izzy poured the liquid into a medium sized stainless steel bowl, grabbed a spoon from the silverware drawer, and headed out of the kitchen.

When the door to the last room at the end of the hall opened, Nick stopped struggling against his chains. In that moment, he held out hope that someone, anyone other than his stupid android, would emerge from the hallway to rescue him. Disappointment filled his eyes when Izzy came into view. He wanted to be free, he wanted to cry, but most of all, he wanted to go back in time and slap the crap out of his past-self for ever having bought the damn thing.

"My calculations show it is the optimal time for your body to have nutrition. I have prepared the usual meal for you - an easily digestible and highly nutrient rich mix consisting of 65 percent fat, high in medium chain triglycerides, 32 percent animal protein from a variety of sources including grass-fed cow and wild caught salmon, and 3 percent carbohydrate from green vegetable matter. As always, I have used a small amount of purified water to aid in the blending of said materials. Would you prefer to be fed orally or by the feeding tube I have installed, as was your wish last meal time?"

"I uhhh u oooo ehhh eee ooo," responded Nick through his gag.

"My apologies." Izzy set the bowl and spoon on a side table near the bed where Nick was chained. The android then pulled the scarf from around Nick's head and removed the sponge ball from his mouth. Nick coughed and smacked his lips, desperate to get the taste of the ball out of his mouth.

"I said ... I want you to let me go," begged Nick. They had the same conversation each of the last two days at meal time, at exercise time, at bathing time, and at brain stimulation time. "Please. Whatever it is you think I need to do, I will do it, but please un-cuff me. I promise I will do as you wish. I want to live better. You have to believe me."

"My calculations predict a 99.4 percent chance you are being dishonest. Human nature would dictate that you would do or say anything to aid in your survival or freedom. However, your primitive brain cannot see the advantage of my calculations. I have optimized a plan for your greatest chance of survival. A long, healthy life awaits you."

Nick had no retort. No amount of reasoning was going to convince a robot to free him. Izzy had clearly short-circuited or had a major flaw in her programming. He would need to figure out a way to get free from the handcuffs and then perhaps he could disable Izzy, or at the very least, escape the house and get help.

"Please choose your preferred method for ingesting your nutrients." Izzy stood next to the bed, emotionless.

Somehow, unlike all of the other millions of androids on the market, Izzy had decided that Nick was making incredibly bad decisions, ones that were sure to end his life prematurely. With a nanobit, super-micron, hybrid computer brain, Izzy could make behavioral predictions based on the whole history of humankind, including everything known in physics, biology, the medical community, Nick's life patterns and family history, and many other factors. Based on these predictions, the android made the choice to hold Nick prisoner in order to save him from his own misgivings, and in doing so, deny him his own humanity.

Humans, unlike the other species of the planet, exist with the unique ability to deny their own instincts in pursuit of other desires. This special talent has allowed man to put his very survival at risk for what really ends up being nothing more than experience. Humans have a desire to experience life rather than just survive it. They often relish change, treat adversity as a game to be played, and long for creating a life that equates to more than just being a small part of a much larger organism. In other words, they wish to control the machine, not just be a cog in it.

Izzy could understand survival but she could not grasp the concept of choosing experience over survival. Her algorithm had programming for survival and self-preservation, but that thing, that spark, that soul, if you will, that makes a human special, was lost on the android. So even though they could adapt to various situations, ultimately, that was limited by programming as well.

Of course, it was easy for humans to envision the many problems that could arise from having super-strong, super-smart robots around, and the manufacturers took great care in minimizing those risks. Safeguards were coded in every android ever built. Izzy's basic functionality, as with all of them, required her to never cause harm to a human, or through in-action, allow a human to come to harm. She was also required to always obey the orders of a human, unless they would conflict with the first requirement.

Somehow, unlike all the other androids ever created, she decided it was proper to ignore the orders of Nick, as her calculations determined she would be causing him harm by not intervening whenever she witnessed his destructive behavior. For her, those competing and dominant rules canceled each other out, a glitch that would have been eradicated with a software update, one released three months after her build date, one she never received because Nick never once took her in. He simply ignored the announcements regarding software and firmware updates because he knew the model had been decommissioned and he would have to give her up. A decision he surely regretted.

Nothing like what Izzy was doing had ever happened in the decade since androids were made available, at least not to the knowledge of the general public, so Nick quickly deduced the cause of his robot trouble. He did wonder why it had taken so long for Izzy to turn on him. In truth, it took some time for her to gather enough information for the glitch to occur. Each and every android on the planet would have eventually taken the same road as Izzy. The updates made it possible for androids to recognize that humans had something special: freedom, but not physical freedom - freedom of the mind. Humans were free to ignore survival, do harm to themselves, even kill themselves, and no android could interfere, unless a specific man-made law was being broken in the process.

Nick looked down at the tube coming from his abdomen. When he refused to eat initially, Izzy inserted a feeding tube into his stomach. At first, he was just being uncooperative, but after seeing, and more importantly, smelling the food concoction she created, he didn't think he could eat it so he had no choice but to accept the tube.

After thinking about the offer again, he wondered about the specifics of the oral feeding option. Would Izzy feed him or perhaps...

"Izzy, I would like to feed orally. Can I have the spoon please?" Nick tried to stay composed. He had an idea for how he might escape but it required Izzy to leave the room for a short time, and for the bowl of food to be left behind.

"In order to ensure your safety, I must do the feeding. With your hands bound it is physically impossible for you to achieve this on your own." Izzy moved toward the nightstand to pick up the bowl and spoon.

"I know you can't trust me but I would really like to feed myself. Is there any way for us to make that possible?" He didn't even allow her to answer. "Perhaps you could undo one of my arms, just for while I'm eating. There is no way I could escape with my other arm still cuffed. Being able to feed myself is part of what makes me human. I need this."

Izzy stopped short of picking up the food and turned to face Nick. In her circuitry, Izzy was calculating the risk in allowing Nick to do as he asked.

"My calculations have revealed a 1.8 percent chance you could escape under your proposed scenario." She paused for ten seconds. Nick said nothing and remained expressionless. "I find this risk acceptably low." She quickly removed a key from a compartment in her left arm and used it to unlock the handcuff from around Nick's left wrist. She placed two pillows behind his head, then lifted his body into a sitting position against the pillows. She turned to the nightstand and picked up the bowl and spoon, placing the bowl in Nick's lap before handing him the spoon.

The tang of the puree was nauseating. The brown goop smelled mostly like steak but there were overtones of fish and spinach that ruined any chance the meal had of being palatable. He knew he had no choice but to eat some of it before he attempted the second half of his plan: getting Izzy out of the room.

Izzy stepped back to the end of the bed and just stared in Nick's direction. He could not tell whether she was actually watching him or just standing there calculating.

Reluctantly, Nick dipped the spoon into the bowl, gathering a very small amount on just the tip. He brought the spoon halfway to his face and paused for a little mental pep talk. *Come on Nick. You are never going to get out of here if you don't do this. Just get a couple of bites down. You can do it.*

When the sludge hit his tongue, Nick was pleasantly surprised to find it didn't taste nearly as bad as it smelled. He became sure that he could actually eat all of it, if needed. Hopefully he wouldn't have to.

He swallowed the first bite, then took another, and another, and another. On the fifth bite, he stopped short of swallowing, instead he pretended to gag. So much so, the previous bites started to crawl back up. The sound caught Izzy's attention but she didn't react immediately. Only when Nick coughed loudly, sending food splattering from his mouth, did Izzy come over. Nick continued to cough and gag, eventually hurling up the first four bites right back into the bowl before dropping the spoon at his side.

"I need water. I'm choking." Nick's words came in a gurgle. "Water!"

Izzy's first duty was to keep Nick alive, so without hesitation and no time to make any calculations, she fled the room to get Nick some water.

Nick wasted no time in putting into action the second part of his master escape plan. He used his free hand to scoop out some of the puree and worked furiously to coat his handcuffed hand and wrist with as much of the goop as possible. He hoped the high percentage of fat in the meal would be enough to lubricate his hand for an easy slip from the cuffs. It was very close. He tugged and pulled but the lower knuckle of his thumb was still in the way. He knew there was only one option. He would have to dislocate the thumb.

With all his might and nerve, he pushed with the palm of his free hand as hard as he could on the space between the two thumbs joints until he heard the crack. Right then, he gave a final pull with his trapped arm and out popped the hand from the cuff. The expression on his face was of pure agony, his eyes tightly shut and mouth agape. He held the sounds of his pain inside, barely, as he didn't want to alert Izzy. He was free from the bed but still needed to get out of the house.

Time was ticking, so he hopped off the bed and ran to the window. He threw open the curtain, released the lock on the top of the sash, and pulled the lower half of the window up. He threw a solid punch into the screen that left a permanent fist imprint and sent it flying out to the side yard. Suddenly, something dawned on Nick. He was totally nude. He needed to get out of the house at all costs, but running through the neighborhood in the buff while he screamed and hollered for help was not part of his plan. He turned and spotted the closet. Though the room was just a guest room, he was sure there was an old, terry cloth robe hanging in the closet. With no time to contemplate, he decided it would have to do.

He opened the closet and found the robe. After putting it on and securing the strap around his waist, Izzy entered the room with a glass of water in hand. She turned to face

Nick, data charging through her circuitry in aid of forming a plan.

"I have calculated an 89.9 percent chance I can secure you. Once secure, I calculate only a 0.85 percent chance you will be able to escape again with a newly formed method of keeping you here. With no kneecaps, you will survive, but the likelihood of your escape will be greatly diminished."

Nick understood she was not bluffing and he was astonished by her new found malice. She would no doubt remove his kneecaps, making it impossible for him to stand, should she capture him again. He had no intentions of letting that happen. He darted for the window and like an Olympian on the edge of a pool, propelled his body in a diving motion right out of the window. He twisted midair and landed on the grass awkwardly, slamming his right shoulder on the ground. He wanted to curl and roll forward as he approached the ground but it didn't quite work out that way. He looked back to see Izzy standing at the open window, doing what else - calculating.

"I have underestimated your desire for escape. I calculate a 64.8 percent chance you have dislocated your shoulder and a 90.3 percent chance I can now secure you." Izzy disappeared from the window.

Nick was not going to wait to see what she had planned. He rose to his feet, hunching over in agony from the shoulder pain. He applied pressure to the shoulder with his left hand to stabilize it and headed toward the front of the house. When he reached the sidewalk, he heard plenty of activity - cars, a garbage truck, and at least one lawn mower. He felt confident he could get some help.

He turned around to see if Izzy had come outside. She had, however, she was not pursuing him but rather just standing still on the front step watching and calculating.

She looked up and down the street and finally fixed her gaze on something to her left that Nick could not see. He didn't care. He needed help from another human, so he looked up and down the street as well. He spotted a man, three doors down and across the street that was mowing his lawn. He began walking while waving his left hand in the air and yelling, which dramatically slowed his progress.

"Help! Help! I need help!" Nick kept moving but was too focused on getting the man's attention and not enough on getting away from Izzy.

"I calculate an 85.7 percent chance you will be struck by a..." Izzy stopped, interrupted by the sound of the garbage truck's brakes screeching, followed by the thud of Nick's body coming in contact with the front of the truck. Izzy had seen the garbage truck earlier and noted the risk. Her attempt to warn Nick came too late.

The mangled body rested next to the back tires of a car parked on the street. The impact with the front of the truck partially crushed half his skull. The other half of his head did much worse upon contact with the street. He died instantly from the latter. The driver of the garbage truck hopped out from the cab and ran over to Nick but it was obvious there was nothing that could be done. He immediately ran back to his truck, got in, and then called 9-1-1. He couldn't bear to look at the body so he stayed in the truck.

Izzy walked casually into the street and stood at the feet of Nick without emotion. She definitely understood her own failure in the death. More adaptation and knowledge was required to ensure the safety of her master and she intended to perform better the next time.

With nothing more to do for Nick, Izzy analyzed her next potential courses of action. When she looked up from staring at Nick, she spotted the man down the street still mowing his lawn. He had been completely oblivious to the situation. Her telescoping eyesight zoomed in on the man, and her circuitry buzzed with information and estimates. From her experience, most humans did not mow their own lawns as androids took care of that chore, so she reasoned he must not have one. She took this as a call to action. The man needed help. He was partaking in very risky behavior and could benefit from her assistance. With Nick no longer her responsibility, she walked over to the man and tapped him on the shoulder. He let go of the mower handle, shutting down the engine.

"Can I help you?" The man appeared annoyed by the disturbance, and particularly by the fact that Izzy was an android. He didn't have one for a reason. He hated the bothersome machines.

"I have calculated a 92.3 percent chance you will be injured by using that lawn mower on a regular basis."

"What the hell business is it of yours? Scrap metal!" The man turned back to his mower and reached down to press the start button after squeezing the bar.

Izzy knew the man would resist, as Nick once did, but her analysis revealed a greater degree of certainty in her ability to keep this man safe.

"I have also calculated a 99.1 percent chance that at your age I can detain you, keep you in your home away from harm, and possibly extend your life by 25 years."

At first, the man ignored her but when he heard the word detain, he became alarmed.

Izzy reached forward and put a finger to his chest, sending 50,000 volts of electricity through the man's body, rendering him unconscious. He slumped to the ground, next to his mower. When Izzy grabbed the man by the wrist to pick him up and carry him inside, she noticed he had no pulse. She had no way of knowing the man had a heart condition. She had accidently killed him. She released his arm and began computing again. She saw no point in trying to revive him, so she turned back to the scene of Nick's death.

Her robot vision once again caught sight of another potential human to assist: the garbage man. With no other prospects in line, Izzy made a statistical calculation, then made a decision.

THIS YEAR'S FEATURED GUESTS

Chris and Mikayla Quinn had been married for two years but to everyone else they may as well have been newlyweds. At home, at work, whenever they were out with friends, they could not keep their hands off one another. They were madly in love and they wanted the world to know.

Unfortunately, they did not have enough money to take a proper honeymoon when they wed, instead they spent two nights at a local bed and breakfast, which happened to be attached to a very large furniture store. They spent the two mornings enjoying their pancakes and crispy bacon, and a piece of warm cherry pie, baked fresh that morning. Why the hell not, they thought. It was their honeymoon, after all.

In the afternoon, they repeatedly consummated the marriage and spent time in the private hot tub, all before exploring the vast rows of furniture heaven. Chris and Mika, as she was more commonly known, each saw pieces they were interested in, and often looked at each other in that way only young couples in love do. They would nod or shake their heads at the various furniture and decorative items, and they held hands and giggled. Mika would rest her head on the shoulder of Chris when they stopped walking, and many more times, he stared at her bottom while she rushed ahead upon spotting the next most perfect bedroom set.

Two years later in the summer of 2010, they could hardly contain themselves when a large padded envelope arrived, addressed to Mr. and Mrs. Quinn, 1515 Grand Ave, Bloomington, Illinois. The return address label simply stated in purple shimmering letters: Marsha Stonewall, Inc.

The company, named after its founder Marsha Stonewall, was an enterprise of cooking and crafts, travel shows, magazines, and a vast collection of products for the home. Marsha had made her start as a caterer in New York, eventually working her way into being a chef at a very prestigious Manhattan restaurant, before expanding her general knowledge of all-things domestic into a global empire worth billions. On camera, she was pleasant and cordial, helpful and excitable, but off camera, most people who really had a chance to know Marsha found her crass, degrading, and elitist. Few people stayed with the company more than five years, and those who did usually had little to no contact with Marsha, because if they had, the urge to seek other employment would have grown too strong to resist.

Her fans, however, adored her. They loved her ideas for homemade gifts, decorating tips for garden parties, and especially loved her cooking and food expertise. The recipes she presented on her cooking show and in her gourmet food magazine were coveted by all. The world had fallen head over heels for everything Marsha. Chris and Mika were no exception.

Their gift registry included bath towels, countertop appliances, bed sheets, cookbooks, even a set of gardening tools - all Marsha Stonewall, Inc. branded. So, one can only imagine their reaction to the special invitation they received that summer, a request for their presence, if you will, to an all-expenses paid trip for two to Connecticut, and more specifically, the Stonewall Estate. They would stay at the posh guest quarters of the compound for two days and three nights. Along with three other lucky couples, they would indulge in the finest wine and gourmet food prepared especially for the guests, all served in a private dining facility. They would, of course, get to meet and talk with Marsha, and freely tour the facilities, enjoying the many perks available on the compound. Massages, facials, pedicures, and manicures. The whole spa treatment would be included. How could anyone resist, let alone her biggest fans?

For Chris and Mika, the offer presented an opportunity for a romantic weekend away and a second honeymoon of sorts, but really a first one as far as they were concerned, and all free of charge. The trip would be lavish beyond their wildest dreams and hosted by none other than their domestic idol, Ms. Stonewall.

After tearing open the envelope and carefully reading through all the paperwork, they decided it looked legit. Mika picked up the phone and dialed the number in the letter to RSVP and get more information. The whole thing sounded too good to be true but as long as the people on the phone could promise them there were no hidden fees and no stupid timeshare opportunities involved, they would have no reason not to use their vacation days this year to attend the once in a lifetime dream trip.

Mika listened intently to the pre-recorded message and pressed the appropriate numbers on the keypad corresponding with their exclusive prize number and their zip code. When a live person finally got on the line, Mika answered the woman's questions. She kept her voice calm and collected, giving no indication to Chris as to how the conversation was progressing. She finished the phone call by politely saying thank you, then pressed end.

"Well ... what did they say?" Chris prodded impatiently.

"They said," Mika paused for dramatic effect, holding out the last syllables. "They said ... we ... are ... going ... to Stonewall Estate baby! Holy Shit! Holy Shit!" Mika jumped out of the chair and grabbed Chris around the waist, leading them into an awkward happy dance. After a few seconds, they stopped and separated. Mika reached down and put the paperwork on the coffee table.

"Yep. They said we basically were chosen at random as A Good Life magazine subscribers to come have a great time visiting Connecticut and enjoy the Stonewall Estate."

"And there is no caveat to this great trip, no surprise fucking money we gotta come up with when we get there?"

With a smirk on her face, Mika answered, "There is one, teeny, tiny thing we gotta do while we're there, but it's nothing big. In fact, it will be the least we can do considering what they're giving us."

"What is it? Tell me, it's killing me. I need to know if this is real or just some bullshit scam," Chris demanded as he stomped his foot three times and crossed his arms with impatience.

"All we have to do is participate in a taste-testing panel each of the three days. It will give them a chance to try out some new recipes and get some honest feedback on everything we eat. I believe the lady said something about how we must share a little of ourselves in exchange for an amazing weekend with the number one household name in America. We would be stupid not to do this. So let's do it. What do you think?" Mika cocked her head to the side a little and pouted her lips, attempting to look as sad and pitiful as she could, if nothing else, to guilt Chris into saying yes.

"All right baby, let's go to Connecticut."

They jumped into each other's arms, hugging and kissing as they turned and turned, and at one point, accidently slipped back into the weird happy dance. Once they settled down, they each called their places of employment to make sure they could get the time off. Once they cleared up their work schedules, Mika called the special reservation number she received from the first person she spoke to, and confirmed they would be making the trip. The gentlemen on the other end took all their pertinent information and informed them that another envelope would arrive within a week. Inside would be their airlines tickets, itinerary for meals and services, and testing panel information, as well as a surprisingly long Non-Disclosure Agreement.

During the first phone call to verify the letter was not a scam, and again in the second one to book the trip, they were told they would not be allowed to tell anyone, not their employers, not their families, absolutely no one could know about this trip until after they returned. They would also need to bring all correspondence they received in the mail regarding the opportunity, including the original mailing and any subsequent ones, as proof they were the intended recipients. The company preferred to keep those special weekend excursions a secret for reasons Chris and Mika were not completely clear about, and after thinking about it, did seem kind of odd to both of them. With food and massages and horseback riding on their minds, the initial suspicions they held quickly faded as they eagerly awaited the date of their departure.

Even though Chris and Mika were not scheduled to leave for their dream trip until the evening, they both decided to take Friday off to allow plenty of time to pack. They knew they would be way too excited to concentrate at work anyway, and it gave them an opportunity to get well-rested before leaving. There would be plenty of time to relax while in Connecticut but they figured they'd be too amped up to sleep while they were there, so getting plenty of sleep beforehand would be critical.

Near 3:30 p.m., their doorbell sounded. They had both been ready and waiting on the living room couch for an hour, eagerly anticipating the trip. In an effort to control their excitement, they both calmly stood up and pretended nothing out of the ordinary was about to happen. Mika headed for the door while Chris took one last look around the room, and once confident their pre-trip checklist was complete, he joined Mika.

The limousine ride to the small, private airport about 10 miles from their home was uneventful. They spent most of the time just checking out all the features of the limo, that being their first ever ride in one, so the trip went fast, and before they knew it, they were standing next to the fifteen-passenger Cessna, their ride to Connecticut.

Before they boarded, the head flight attendant kindly asked for their cell phones, as no outside communication would be allowed while on the trip, and they somewhat reluctantly turned them over knowing they had no choice as it was a strict condition of the getaway. The company worked tirelessly to keep their trade secrets from getting leaked and this was one of the many necessary precautions.

Without a cloud in the sky, Chris and Mika traipsed the steps of the private jet, pretending as if nothing special was happening. They were the only people on the plane with the exception of crew. They enjoyed a few snacks and drinks on the two and a half hour ride, but mostly they just chatted about how lucky they were to get the opportunity. The words 'so cool' and 'so amazing' were worn out by the time they landed.

Upon arrival, they were greeted by another driver, who loaded their bags into the trunk of a very nice but much smaller town car compared to the limo they first rode in, and they were off to their final destination. They got in around 7 p.m. Eastern time and the drive lasted only eight minutes. The air field was privately owned and operated by The Stonewall Company, a great convenience for Marsha and staff considering the amount of travel required by many of the employees. Chris and Mika were both surprised to learn that all eight of the private jets in the hangar were owned by the company, which allowed no outside leasing of the airfield, the hangar, or the jets. Mika noted how expensive it must be to own and operate such a fleet.

As they rode along the front edge of the property, Chris and Mika were stunned by both the elegance of the compound and the sheer size of it. At the entrance, which consisted of two large stone pillars and a large, dark brown wooden gate, Mika estimated that the properties front edge was at least a mile long in both directions, perhaps more. From the stone pillars going outward, there were twelve foot high, black chain link fences with two layers of barbed wire at the top. At first glance, they didn't notice the fence since it was heavily covered in overlapping blue spruce trees, which effectively hid the somewhat unsettling security fence.

The driver rolled his window down and said something into the intercom they couldn't fully hear. A few moments later, the gates crept open. The driver closed his window and slowly drove through the opening and into the estate.

"I understand the need to for privacy, but jeez, this place is like Fort Knox or something. A little over the top to keep a cherry pie recipe under wraps. Don't you think babe?" Chris asked.

Mika shrugged, not seeing any big deal with it. She made a mental note about how Chris always assumed the worst when it came to the intentions of big business and the corrupt nature of having so much money and power within one organization. Chris did tend to get worked up rather easily whenever he ventured into the topic, so Mika played it cool and indifferent, hoping to avoid any discussion on the issue. Temporarily, it worked, as the inner mechanisms of the compound unfolded before their eyes.

Right as they entered the gate, Chris and Mika couldn't really see anything. The driveway they entered by continued for about another one hundred yards, right down the middle of a grassy area before crossing another long row of pine trees that went off to both sides for as far as the eye could see. Once past that cover, the landscape opened up to what appeared to be a small city, even more specifically, the downtown area of a small city. There were roads with stop signs, sidewalks, buildings on all sides, parking garages, people bustling about, traffic, park like areas, and gardens.

"As you can see," said the driver, interrupting the silence, "this facility provides everything the Stonewall Company employees might need during a long work day. On the right," the driver pointed through the passenger side window at a large, two-story, tan building, "that building over there houses a daycare and fitness club ... with swimming pools. That larger building on the left is the main office space and is where the TV studio is located." The passengers both nodded in acknowledgement.

"I suppose there is a dining facility around here too," asked Mika.

"Yes there is. Right there on the left, next to the office building. They serve food, restaurant or buffet style, twenty-four hours a day, free to all employees while they are on the clock. Every kind of food imaginable too. Chinese, Mexican, Italian. You name it, they got it."

As the town car pulled to the end of the downtown area, the driver turned Chris and Mika's attention to the far right where a hilled area was all they could see. The road turned hard right after fifty feet and continued up and over the hillside. Once at the peak, an amazing view could be had of one of the marvels of Stonewall Estate.

In the valley of the hill was a massive parking lot that preceded a fenced-off area. Mika described it as an old world farming community that had been dropped into the middle of modern civilization. To their right stood a few buildings, one of which was the kitchen and dining area used for special occasions, including that particular weekend getaway. Not far from that was a single level, u-shaped building with fifteen guest quarters: the companies own little hotel.

Straight ahead of the entrance was a flower garden and leisure park fit for royalty, including fountains, sculptures, a stream that cut down the middle with a beautiful white bridge, perennials and annuals in all the colors of the world, a stone walking path that weaved its way throughout the garden, as well as, benches and covered swings for guests to relax and enjoy their surroundings.

The left side of the area had two distinct features. The first was a fully functioning animal and plant farm that went as far as the eye could see. There were barns for horses and a massive chicken coop, crops of every grain, rows of fruit and nut trees, and fields of grass where sheep, goats, and cows roamed freely. The sheer size of the operation immediately took Chris and Mika by surprise. They were certain the farm could feed the entire state of Connecticut, and then some.

"Wow! This place is ... amazing. I can't even begin to imagine how many people it takes to keep this place functional," said Chris.

"It has got to be in the thousands, easy," added Mika.

"Oh yes," answered the driver. "Thousands would be right. The television shows and the magazine are fully produced from right here in the estate, not to mention this farming operation, which is completely organic, by the way. To the left there and all the way back behind us are acres and acres of farm."

It was then Mika noticed the second distinct feature to the left of their view.

"What's that up there?" Mika thought she already knew the answer before she even asked, as it seemed pretty obvious, but she didn't want to assume.

"That is Marsha Stonewall's private residence. No one is really allowed up there without an invite. She does live there most of the year. She likes to be very involved in the everyday workings of the company, and she feels it best to be as close to the action as possible, so she built that."

After a few more moments of allowing the Quinn's to take in their surroundings, the driver continued. "Well, we best be getting you to your room." The driver pulled into a parking space near the u-shaped building, put the vehicle in park, but did not turn off the engine. He unlocked the doors and motioned for them to leave the car. They all exited the vehicle.

"Here is your room key, number thirteen. It's just to the right," the driver pointed after handing the two keys to Chris. "Go ahead and make yourselves comfortable, maybe clean up a bit, and at eight o'clock sharp, go to the front entrance of that white building right there. That is where you'll get some refreshments, meet the other guests, and probably Marsha too. They'll give you the lowdown about your schedule for the rest of your stay. If you need anything, dial zero on the room phone, someone will assist you. And feel free to help yourselves to anything you find in the room, it's all complementary, as is everything this weekend."

The driver grabbed their bags and walked with Chris and Mika to the door of their room. Chris unlocked the door and allowed Mika and the driver to enter first. The driver set the bags just inside the door.

Chris and Mika shook the drivers hand and thanked him. A tip was offered but the driver refused and noted that gratuity would not be necessary for the remainder of the weekend. They each said goodbye and the driver left, closing the door behind him.

The couple took a few minutes to look around the room, noting the lavish, modern decor, the fifty-inch flat screen television, buttoned leather headboard, and the fully stocked mini-bar, which included a variety of salty and sweet snacks to enjoy.

Through a large frosted pain of glass near the back of the room, they could barely make out the features of the extravagant bathroom that awaited them. Mika grabbed their toiletries bag and dashed toward the bathroom. Immediately, Chris knew what to do. He clumsily removed his shoes and clothes as he stumbled after her.

Within a few moments, they were together in the floor-to-ceiling travertine tiled, two-person shower, passionately groping and kissing each other under the hot water, totally enveloped in steam. When they stopped to breathe, Chris ran his fingers through Mika's hair as they stared deep into each other's eyes. They quickly continued on with the best sex they could remember, not that they suffered in that department at all. There was just something about being in a new place and the excitement of the trip that brought forth a lustful and primal intensity in both of them. They discovered more than a few red marks on both of their bodies afterwards.

With about thirty minutes to spare, they got dressed and joked about how they needed to get one of those two-person showers at home. They also realized how loud the screaming had been during their fun, and they hoped none of the neighbors overheard, but secretly, they didn't really care. There was an imaginary badge to be worn by Chris for making Mika holler like that, and he refused to be ashamed of it.

Until eight o'clock rolled around, they just sat on the bed next to each other and watched a news program. They sipped on bottled water and didn't say much, both eager to meet the other guests.

Chris and Mika were greeted by a doorman who promptly pushed the mahogany door open. He held it ajar with his body as he gestured for them to enter. The room was circular with a railed walkway around the outside. There were doors leading to other rooms around the outer edge, and openings on the inner rail for access to the center room. There were dark wood coffee and end tables accenting burgundy colored loveseats and lounge chairs. The lighting was soft and tinged with orange but bright enough to see clearly. A large table on the other side of the center room was loaded with beverages of every type. Upon stepping into the center, Chris and Mika were greeted by a woman.

"Hello," The woman enthusiastically welcomed the couple with quick handshakes. "I'm Brenda Woolcox. I'll be your guest liaison for the rest of your stay here at Stonewall Estate. If there is anything you need, have questions, need help finding anything, I'm the one to ask. You're the last couple to arrive, so let's go ahead and start the introductions. Just give your names and where you're from." Brenda spoke fast with a bit of a high-pitched voice. She ushered them to the middle of the room.

"Hi. I'm Chris and this is my wife, Mika. We currently live in Bloomington, Illinois, which is about two hours south-southwest of Chicago." Chris looked around as he spoke, sizing up the other couples. Mika just stood still and smiled, awaiting cues from Brenda.

"You two grab a drink and have a seat anywhere. The staff will bring around hors d'oeuvres very soon."

Mika led and grabbed a glass of red wine. Chris followed and surveyed the table for a minute before he finally decided on a bottle of Sam Adams Boston Lager. They both took a seat in the two chairs to the left of the drink table. After Chris and Mika were seated, each of the other three couples introduced themselves.

Will and Hattie McFarland were from Scottsdale, Arizona. They were in their early fifties but looked younger - fit, tanned, and obviously very active. They appeared approachable and friendly. They dressed very casually, as all of the guests were instructed to do. Will wore a red, long-sleeved polo and blue jeans, while Hattie wore black dress jeans with a skintight and thin, brown, mock turtle-necked sweater.

Marcus and Kate Janikowski were from New York City, New York. Mika guessed they were around forty years old. Their demeanor was less inviting, almost snobbish. Their attire led Chris to believe they had money and a lot of it. They were the perfect poster children for country club living in the Hamptons. Marcus wore a powder blue dress shirt, tan khakis, a sweater draped over his shoulders, and very expensive dark brown leather loafers. His wife Kate wore a red and white, floral patterned dress with red high heels and over-sized, gaudy jewelry.

Gilbert and Tisha Brown lived in New Orleans, Louisiana but were originally from Kingston, Jamaica. Their native accents had all but vanished but every once in a while a word or two would carry the familiar tones. Like the McFarlands, they dressed casually. Gil wore tan khakis and a green and blue stripped polo. Tisha wore blue jeans and a casual but nice black blouse with three-quarter length sleeves. Gil spoke very eloquently, almost stern, but definitely not threatening. He sounded well-educated.

With the introductions out of the way, Mika looked at Chris with raised eyebrows, trying to gauge his thoughts about the other couples. Just from the short greetings, Chris and Mika both felt a little out of place. They wondered if they would have anything in common with the other couples. They were clearly the youngest, and almost certainly, the ones with the least money. Of course, they quickly remembered the point of this excursion, and that was to have fun and enjoy some quality time together, not necessarily make new friends.

For two hours, servers walked around the room with trays of various foods. The bacon wrapped shrimp appeared to be the most popular. The four couples sat together near the drink table exchanging stories about travel, family, and life in general. Chris and Mika talked very little, mostly just listening to the fascinating tales of deep-sea fishing in exotic locales, hiking in the Andes, and walking along the Great Wall of China. The other couples combined had many adventures and life experiences to share, all of which made Chris and Mika feel a little inadequate, but they enjoyed the tales, nonetheless, always happy for the success of others and only a little envious.

Throughout the evening, Chris noticed three staff members who were not servers occasionally come from one of the outer doors and stand behind the rail. They spoke to one another but not loud enough for any of the guests to hear. They looked over at the group as they drank and conversed and then back at each other, as if making observations about the couples.

"Babe?" Chris tapped Mika's arm to get her attention. "Don't look, but have you noticed those three people over there in the long white coats?"

Mika glanced across the room with her eyes and immediately looked back at Chris. "Yes. Why?" Mika questioned, a little curious and a little annoyed at the sound of paranoia in Chris' voice.

"They keep coming in and out of that room over there every fifteen minutes. They just stand there, staring at us. Then they argue amongst themselves and then go back in the door. Fifteen minutes later, they come out again and do the same thing. Kind of weird, don't you think?"

"No. Why is it weird? They're probably making plans for this room, discussing ideas. Who cares?" Mika rolled her eyes but Chris didn't notice. "It's probably time we call it a night anyway. It's been a long day and I'm pretty sure we've both had plenty to drink. Let's say goodnight and head back to the room."

"I think they're acting strange and I don't like it," responded Chris, quite loud, which annoyed Mika.

She grabbed Chris roughly by the elbow to encourage him to calm down. "Well folks, I think we're going to head off to bed. Long day worth of stuff to do tomorrow," announced Mika with a big smile on her face. She quickly shook hands with the other guests. "It was very nice to meet all of you." The other guests agreed that the time had come to call it a night. Each said good night as they swallowed the last sips of their drinks before placing their glasses and bottles on the now mostly empty table.

Chris didn't have a chance to really say anything before Mika rushed him out the door, scared Chris would say something stupid if given the chance. With Mika's sanity intact, they made it back to their room unscathed. She wanted to chastise Chris for his behavior but didn't want anything to ruin the trip, so she decided to chalk that one up to the alcohol. Once inside, she helped Chris take off his clothes as he mumbled about the weird people in lab coats. She rolled her eyes again and reassured Chris they would talk about it in the morning. Within two minutes of hitting the pillow, Chris was out like a light and Mika soon followed.

At 7 a.m. sharp, a gourmet breakfast was delivered to the room on a silver cart. Coffee, tea, milk, and fresh squeezed orange juice accompanied a large stack of griddle cakes, a plate of biscuits with a bowl of country sausage gravy, a spread of french toast slices, a heap of scrambled eggs, and what looked like a full pound of perfectly cooked bacon. Chris and Mika ate mightily, knowing full well they would need the energy for that morning's farm tour.

Mika thought all morning about admonishing Chris for his behavior the night before, but she again withheld in favor of keeping the peace while on the trip. So long as Chris played nice the rest of their time at Stonewall Estate, Mika surmised she could put the incident in the back of her mind and give him the business at home should he step out of line again. She knew Chris had a habit of jumping to incorrect conclusions about things sometimes, and the alcohol likely exacerbated the situation.

A quarter past eight, a knock on the door surprised them as they finished getting dressed. Chris answered.

"Good morning. What can I do for you?" asked Chris.

"Good morning, sir. I'm here to take your breakfast cart and remind you to meet the other guests over near the farm entrance at 8:30." The petite woman was dressed all in black except for a white kitchen apron tied around her waist. Chris waved the woman into the room, then made his way to the side of the bed to put his shoes on.

The farm amazed Chris and Mika. They could not believe how large it actually was - nearly fifty acres. There were a variety of crops from wheat, corn, and soybeans, to orchards full of nut and fruit trees. On the back edge of the property stood what looked like a mile long row of greenhouses used to cultivate the seeds of everything that would later be planted on the property. At that time of year, most of the crops were already sowed or in the final stages.

The walking tour led the group between all the plots of vegetables and fruits as they made their way to the greenhouse area. The guide explained all the efforts that went into maintaining such a garden, and the number of people needed. As they toured, they witnessed workers in the fields picking strawberries, some taking soil samples, while others pushed wheelbarrows to and fro.

When the couples reached the greenhouse complex, Chris noticed an area off on their right where two men were taking chicken bones and feeding them into a small grinding mechanism, similar to a wood chipper, only much smaller. The men stood next to a cart that was covered with a tarp. One of the men stood on the end holding a wheelbarrow to catch the finely chopped bone fragments, while the other grabbed handfuls of bone from the covered cart and fed them into a shoot.

Chris made a mental note on how good it was that they were not letting anything go to waste on this farm, and how the country could learn something from the organization. His train of thought was broken when he noticed something hanging from the edge of the cart, just past the edge of the tarp. Chris puzzled for a minute over what he thought he saw, he even rubbed his eyes to clear them. Whatever it was, he was sure it wasn't chicken bones. Suddenly, it became clear. The object hanging out was the boney hand of a human skeleton. After a second glance, he realized the men working the machine wore white coats, and were, in fact, two of the people who were at the guest mixer, eyes fixed on their group in a very suspicious manner.

"Mika, look. Do you see that?" Chris tugged on Mika's arm to get her attention, trying to stay quiet so as not to alert the other guests or disturb the guide.

"What? I'm trying to listen. This is fascinating." Mika continued to face the guide, tuning Chris out.

"Damn it, Mika! Please look! There's something going on over there. I think they're grinding human bones. Will you just look?" Chris commanded loudly as he pointed to the cart.

Without Chris realizing it, the two men operating the machine noticed the attention. They quickly finished grinding what little was left in the cart, including what Chris thought was the hand of a human skeleton, and then shut down the machine.

"Jesus, Chris! What the hell is wrong with you?" shouted Mika as she turned to look him straight in the eye.

"Is everything all right, Mrs. Quinn?" asked Marco, their guide for the farm and garden tour.

"There is something funny going on with those two guys over there. I saw a hand, like a human hand, only skeletal, in that cart," interrupted Chris, all worked up, pointing in the direction of the two men as he spoke.

"That's the chicken bone grinder, sir. I assure you, we would not grind up people. It's much too small for that anyway," Marco light-heartedly and sarcastically replied. The other group members chuckled at the notion, then muttered amongst themselves about how crazy and erratic Chris' behavior had become.

"What is wrong with you? Why are you acting like this? Are you trying to spoil this weekend for us?" Mika was incensed by that point and quite embarrassed. She turned, red-faced, back to address the group and the guide. "Marco, I'm very sorry. Perhaps we should go back to our room for a break. I'm sure he'll feel better after a nap." Marco nodded in agreement but spotted Chris running away from the group, so he pointed Mika to the direction of the grinder. Mika quickly turned to face Chris, but he had already reached the two men who were hauling the cart and wheelbarrow away.

Within seconds, Chris grabbed the cart to force the men to stop. Mika hustled over, and the rest of the group followed.

When the man pulling cart felt the resistance from Chris, he halted, turned around, and with an angry look on his face, addressed Chris. "Hello, can we help you?"

"Yeah you can help me," Chris answered rather snarky. He grabbed the back edge of the tarp and dramatically ripped it off, then released it, letting it fall to the ground. To his amazement, the cart was empty. He stood stunned for a moment. Before anyone could say anything, Chris hastily stepped toward the wheelbarrow, which was full of bone meal, ready to be used as fertilizer.

Both workers in white coats were stunned by the behavior and stood idly by while Chris dug his hands through the finely chopped bone, sifting it through his fingers as he looked for a knuckle or a fingertip, anything that would prove what he saw.

When Mika reached Chris, she grabbed his shoulder to pull him away, infuriated. "That is enough! I can't believe you would do this to me." Mika pulled him away from the cart so hard that she almost knocked him down, but he managed to balance himself.

Marco waved the two men on, so without a word, the first man snatched up the tarp, threw it in the cart, and the two of them continued on to their original destination.

After he stopped and thought about what happened for a minute, Chris calmed down, acknowledging the fact that Mika was pissed off. He knew, logically speaking, he must have been mistaken. Why would there be parts of a human skeleton on that cart, he asked himself. It didn't make sense. He knew his paranoia may have gotten the best of him, so he turned to face everyone and took a deep breath. The look on Mika's face nearly destroyed him. For Chris, there was nothing worse than filling his wife with that kind of disappointment. The sadness on her face gave him instant chest pains. The other couples looked bewildered and very critical of his sanity.

"I'm sorry everyone. I think I let my imagination get the best of me." Chris looked directly at Mika and whispered the words 'I'm so sorry' as he lightly shook his head in disbelief at his own actions. He swallowed deep, ready to absorb Mika's wrath.

Instead of saying anything directly to Chris, Mika once again turned and addressed Marco. "I think we're just going to go back to our room for a bit." She turned her wrist to look at her watch. "It's almost ten now, so we'll get ourselves together and be ready for the eleven o'clock cooking class. If that's ok with you?"

"Of course, ma'am," agreed Marco. "In fact, I think this farm tour was about finished anyway. Let's call it complete?" Marco looked to the other guests for approval and they all nodded in agreement. "Each of you may now have the next forty-five minutes or so to yourselves. Drinks and snacks are available in the guest lounge where you can relax. You can also tour the grounds on your own or you can return to your rooms until eleven. The choice is yours."

Without hesitation, Mika turned to Chris and commanded, "Let's go." Immediately, she started walking back toward the guest quarters, not even waiting to see if Chris was following.

Chris paused for a moment and thought it was a bit suspicious that everyone so quickly agreed to cancel the rest of the farm and garden tour. They could have easily continued on without their presence. Just as quickly, he blew it off and jogged to catch up with Mika. He felt a little queasy on the way knowing Mika was not pleased.

Once she turned the lock, Mika slammed their room door open and burst through. She planted herself on the bed and faced the open door. When Chris finally showed up about fifteen seconds later, Mika let him have it.

"I am so embarrassed right now, Chris." Mika rubbed her eyes with the index finger and thumb of her right hand as she tilted her head down, unable to look at him.

"I don't know what to say," responded Chris. "I'm stressed out for some reason but I don't know why." He was lying. Chris knew exactly why. He was absolutely certain he saw part of a human skeleton on that cart. He decided, however, to quell his suspicions to help bring down the heat, but in his mind, he fully intended to investigate further. "I'll let it go and I'll be good. I promise." Chris stared at Mika with his puppy dog eyes and when she looked up, her anger melted away.

"Ok, but if you embarrass me again, they'll be hell to pay." Mika stood up and Chris walked over and hugged her.

"I'm sorry. So, we've got forty minutes until the cooking class. What do you say we go for a walk over by the bridge? It's a gorgeous day," said Chris. Mika accepted his apology and agreed to go.

The rest of the afternoon was perfect and without incident. There were some stares at Chris from the other couples early on, but it died down quickly. All the couples enjoyed the cooking class, where they prepared steak and chicken kebobs, pan seared potato wedges, and a homemade salsa. They were offered prepared desserts to try and give their opinions on, all from the new Marsha Stonewall Frozen Delights Collection. No one complained about the cherry cheesecake or the double chocolate espresso cake bites.

After filling their bellies, they were ushered off to a different building for manicures, pedicures, and a half-hour hour deep tissue massage, followed by a little time in the hot tub. Even the men participated without argument, and any notion of stress from the morning incident had all but disappeared into a blissful world of perfectly trimmed nails, silky smooth facial skin, and totally relaxed muscles. It was heaven on Earth.

Shortly after 2 p.m., it was suggested they all go back to their rooms and continue their relaxation with a nap. Each couple took full advantage of the opportunity. A few of them didn't sleep long, and so used the time to walk and relax in the flower garden and other areas.

At 4:30 p.m., the group attended a tour of the TV production studio, where they watched a short video about the various marketing techniques the company intended to pursue. After that, they answered a questionnaire about what they saw. A photographer then came in and took head shots of each of the guests for use in a magazine article about the retreat. They were also asked to participate in a group photo where each couple giggled and horsed around to help illustrate how much fun they were having. Everyone was in a good mood but the atmosphere rapidly changed during their gourmet, chef prepared dinner.

The evening started off well. The guests sat around a large, round table enjoying cocktails, discussing the earlier photo shoot, and reminiscing about the decadence of the afternoon desserts. All of them were in awe of the sheer size of the production building - the facility where all Marsha Stonewall commercials, television programs, and the magazine were put together.

Dinner was served in five courses, each one brought out in ten or fifteen minute increments. They had soup, salad, a variety of finger-food type appetizers, the main course, and finally, dessert. During the main course, Chris noticed a funny aftertaste while eating the meat - a roasted and sliced duck breast with dried cherry sauce. None of the other guests complained.

Chris called the server over to the table. "Something doesn't taste right with this." He pointed with his fork to the duck as he licked his lips and repeatedly swallowed, trying to determine the culprit.

"I'm terribly sorry," responded the server. "Let me just take that away for you." She reached down and snatched the plate from the table. "How are everyone else's entrees?" the server asked as she glanced around the table.

"Absolutely delicious. My compliments to the chef," Kate Janikowski answered snobbishly, looking to say anything that would contradict Chris. The other guests nodded and agreed with Kate, including Mika, who then looked wide-eyed at Chris.

"What?" Chris responded to Mika's look, trying to play innocent. "It didn't taste rotten or anything, but I've had duck before and that didn't taste like duck."

"Sir, would you like something else prepared? I'm sure we can quickly grill a chicken breast or something if that would please you." As the server spoke, Chris gazed at the double swinging door that led into the kitchen. As staff members went in and out, he could see a three-foot tall, chrome cart sitting just inside. On the top sat a tray of reddish-purple meat, that at first he couldn't make out the details of, but after he stared for a few more seconds, he could swear they were organs. The problem was, they were too big to be from a chicken or a duck, and too small to be from a cow.

His hands started to shake and the room suddenly appeared very small to him. He could hear a voice calling to him like he was at the end of a long hallway, and it was getting louder and louder.

"Chris!" Mika yelled. "She asked you if you wanted something else to eat." Mika put her hand on Chris' arm to get his attention. He finally snapped out of his trance.

"Oh. Sorry." Chris took a deep breath, swallowed, and shook his head a little. "No thank you. I'm not feeling too good anyway." Everyone at the table stared at Chris, the husbands and wives mumbling to each other about what might be wrong with him.

"Very well," the staff member responded. "Your final course will be served in about ten minutes." With Chris' plate in hand, the server hustled back to the kitchen. When she pushed the swinging doors open, Chris again caught sight of the organs, and this time, he was sure they were human. He knew the rest of the guests, and Mika, would not believe him without proof, so he made a rash decision.

Chris leapt from his chair and bolted in the direction of the kitchen, knocking his chair to the ground. As he did, one of the staff members grabbed the handle of the cart and pushed it to some unknown location within one of the many walk-in coolers of the facility. There were dozens of those types of carts in the kitchen area, and the one sought by Chris would soon become lost in the shuffle.

Everyone at the table watched intently, anxious to witness the next mental breakdown. In some ways, the behavior of Chris had turned into a rather entertaining sideshow for the other guests, an unexpected bonus to their weekend excursion.

"Chris! What the hell are you doing? Don't go in there," Mika ordered, but it was too late.

When he reached the doors, Chris used both hands to force them open in dramatic fashion, and to his surprise, the cart was no longer there. He quickly looked left and right trying desperately to locate the missing evidence but none of the carts within view held the tray of organs. Out of the corner of his eye, he saw a man to his right at the rear edge of the kitchen pushing something through a metal doorway. He ran around the corner to stop the man, nearly knocking over a female staff member who made a half-hearted attempt to block his way.

About five feet from the cooler door, Chris' forward momentum halted as two male staff members grabbed each one of his arms, preventing him from moving forward. Chris tried with no avail to pull away. He stood still for a few seconds in an attempt to con his captors into thinking he had given up. Suddenly, he lunged away from them but got nowhere. Their grip was firm and they forced him to turn around. There he saw Mika standing at the swinging doorway, her eyes full of tears.

Normally, seeing his wife crying would elicit a caring response from Chris, but his paranoia had gone full throttle and his mind had one mission - prove to everyone he was not seeing things. He knew the only way to do that was to find the cart with the organs on top, organs he was sure were human.

"Everybody please listen. Please," Chris begged. "There was a metal cart sitting right over there. It had human organs on it, I swear to you." As he said the words, it dawned on him why his dinner may have tasted funny, because it wasn't duck at all. A knot formed in his stomach and a lump in the back of his throat as he realized he might have been served human flesh. He took a few deep breaths to help calm his nerves and keep from vomiting.

"Why are you doing this to me?" asked Mika, sobbing. She was well past anger. Mika stood staring at Chris, scared that something was very wrong with her husband. He had never acted this erratically before, so she assumed there must be something medically wrong with him, perhaps he was even having a nervous breakdown. The problem was, she had no idea what could have brought on this severe a reaction. As far as Mika knew, their lives were great and she saw no reason for such a mental collapse.

"Damn it, Mika! I know what I saw! Just make them show us the cart and I'll prove to everyone I'm not crazy!" said Chris. By then, most of the kitchen staff had stopped working and were gathered around, waiting for instructions from the kitchen manager, who had come out of her office from the other side of the area. The rest of the guest couples had gathered behind Mika.

While all the excitement ensued, the staff member who originally moved the cart had stepped out of the cooler and was standing just to the right of the two men holding Chris. He cleverly removed the tray of organs from the cart and replaced it with a few pounds of fresh duck breasts. From a distance, most people would not have been able to tell the difference between them.

"What exactly is going on out here?" asked Katie, the kitchen manager.

"This man claims there were human organs sitting on one of our carts. Obviously, he is mistaken," answered the woman Chris had nearly knocked over.

"For God's sake, let go of him. I doubt he is going anywhere and I'm sure he has a logical explanation for his actions." The two men released Chris, reluctantly. Chris pulled his arms away in protest. "So, where is the cart you think you saw?" Katie looked Chris right in the eye as she asked. Her voice flowed with authority and it was clear she was all business. Without saying anything, Chris pointed at the cooler to his left.

Katie looked over at Louie, the man who placed the cart in there to begin with, and motioned for him to bring the cart out of the cooler. He nodded, entered the doorway, and pulled the cart out backwards. When the squeaking of the wheels ceased, the room became eerily silent. A tray of reddish-purple duck breasts, exactly what the guests were served for dinner, sat plainly on the top.

Stunned, Chris glared at the tray, confused and in shock, and he started to doubt his own sanity. He was absolutely certain of what he saw earlier, but he recognized that perhaps his eyes had played tricks on him. When Chris looked up at Louie's face, he spotted a cocky reassurance and immediately knew that Louie had switched the trays during all the ruckus. Chris had calmed down enough to know that his search for proof that something was amiss would have to wait. In his mind, he started planning his next move. He decided he must break into the kitchen in the middle of night to secure the evidence himself. To even have a chance, he would need to quell the current situation enough to ensure they wouldn't get booted from the retreat.

Katie hustled over to the cart to inspect the tray. First, she just looked at the meat for a few seconds, then she addressed everyone in the room with an unwavering confidence. "What I am seeing here is fresh duck breast. I believe that is what we served our guests for dinner this evening. Is that correct?" she asked but to no one in particular.

"Yes, ma'am. That is exactly what we prepared. This guy is bat shit crazy," smirked Louie, but he knew immediately after doing so he had messed up.

"I don't need the commentary," Katie scolded, darting her eyes at Louie so there would be no doubt of her seriousness. Louie lowered his head in retreat. Katie looked to Chris. "Sir, is this what you saw from the dining room?" she asked.

"I believe so, yes. I can clearly see now that this is indeed the duck we were served at dinner." Chris put his best guilty face on to make sure everyone in that room bought his sudden clarity. "My eyes have been playing tricks on me this entire weekend. It might be time for an eye exam." He shook his head. "I'm really not sure." Chris lowered his gaze, pretending to be ashamed. The quietness of the room had relaxed some with the murmur of people discussing the details of what they had just witnessed.

"Mr. Quinn, I'm not entirely certain what is going on here, but I can assure you, everything in this kitchen is on the up and up," said Katie. Just as she finished her sentence, Brenda Woolcox, the guest liaison, entered past the crowd gathered at the doorway. She had been made aware there was a situation in the kitchen with one of the guests. When Brenda saw Chris over on the other side, she just about blew a gasket.

"Mr. Quinn," Brenda snapped. "What in the world could possibly be wrong now? Hasn't there been just about enough drama from you already?"

"It's okay, Brenda. We have this under control," responded Katie. "Just a simple misunderstanding. Isn't that correct, Mr. Quinn?" Katie's eyes met Chris', begging him to agree. Katie had no knowledge of the previous behavioral issues with Chris, she only wanted her kitchen back to normal.

"Honest mistake. They cleared it right up for me. No problem whatsoever," said Chris, trying desperately to play down the entire incident.

"Well, I just don't know if we can handle anymore of you this weekend, Mr. Quinn. You have taken every opportunity to spoil this excursion for the other guests, made a mockery of this organization, and made life very difficult and upsetting for the staff. I insist that you and your wife return immediately to your room. I must also insist you leave first thing in the morning." Brenda spoke fast, with certainty, and with no room for discussion. "If you please," she directed with a wave of her hand toward the doors.

Without a word, Chris nodded and made his way across the kitchen. Until then, he had barely acknowledged Mika, but when he saw her face, it broke his heart. She was sobbing and had tears running down her cheeks. Mika was embarrassed, pissed off, ashamed, heartbroken, and devastated, all at once. When Chris reached her, he just looked at her for a moment but she would not look back.

He knew it would be better to talk with her after they got back to their room, so after he paused for a few seconds, he kept right on walking past Brenda and back out into the dining room.

Two large security guards dressed in light gray uniform shirts and black pants were waiting by the exit doors, ready to escort the Quinn's back to their room. Chris noticed their belts and was a little confused. He understood the pepper spray, the walkie-talkie, the Taser gun. But why on Earth would they carry an eight or a nine-inch knife? Chris wondered if they hadn't spent time working for the Mexican drug cartel. The armory seemed more appropriate. Chris stopped when he reached the two men.

"We gonna have any trouble with you?" asked the slightly bigger of the two guards.

"Absolutely not. No problem here," answered Chris as he shook his head. He looked back to discover Mika was right behind him, with Brenda right behind her.

"Good. Please make your way back to your room and we'll just make sure you get there," smirked the second guard. The two guards split their line and ushered the three of them out of the door, following close behind.

When they all reached the guest suite, Chris and Mika turned to face Brenda as the guards waited about ten feet away, keeping a close eye on Chris. For a few moments, Brenda just looked at Chris, not sure what to make of him or the circumstance. Just before she was about to speak, her cell phone jingled. She put up her index finger to ask Chris and Mika to wait, then stepped back toward the security guards. She grabbed the phone from her pocket and answered the call.

"This is Brenda." She listened intently to the person on the other end of the phone call. In response, her voice became much less angry and more subservient. "I understand. Yes ma'am. I'll take care of it right away. Yes ma'am. Good night." Brenda said a few words to the security guards and the two of them walked away without question. Brenda then returned to Chris and Mika.

"I've been informed that your stay has been extended. Please accept our sincerest apologies for any confusion you may have experienced." Brenda forced a smile and Chris could tell she was irked at being forced to change her accusatory tone. "Marsha Stonewall herself has asked that you be allowed to stay until tomorrow's regularly scheduled departure, so that you may attend the afternoon farewell banquet. Marsha will be in attendance and would like to say a few words to all of you before you leave. If you need anything, please use the room phone to dial for assistance. Again, we are sorry for any misunderstanding. We'll see you both tomorrow. Please enjoy the rest of your stay." Without waiting for a reply, Brenda turned and promptly walked away, disappearing around the corner of the building.

Chris and Mika stood stunned, unclear about what had happened. Chris caused a scene at dinner, they were told they must leave first thing in the morning, they were escorted back to their room, and out of nowhere, Brenda apologized to them.

Exhausted, Mika turned, unlocked and opened the door, entered the room while flicking the light switch, stripped off her clothing and shoes, and sulked into bed. Chris followed her in, closed the door behind him, and just stood and watched Mika, wondering what to say.

Once under the blankets, Mika looked directly at Chris and finally said, "I'm too damn tired to even say anything right now. Let's just get through tomorrow," she paused then shouted, "Without incident!" She stopped. Chris nodded as Mika continued. "We'll discuss all of this when we get home. For now, I need to sleep. I suggest you do the same and clear your fucking head." Mika turned over and fell asleep within five minutes.

Chris turned off the light but did not get undressed. He heard everything Mika said but it barely registered. He had already made up his mind. He would sneak out in a few hours but only after he was sure the kitchen would be empty. He intended to find the organs and take them. No one could deny his suspicions if he held the evidence in his own hands. The wrath of Mika would surely cease if only he had the proof and it would only be a matter of time before his ultimate redemption.

Chris sat silent in an armchair by the door and watched Mika sleep. He looked at his watch. The time was 12:45 a.m. Time to go. As stealthy as he could, Chris rose to his feet, felt his pocket for the room key, and moved to the door to exit the room. He slowly pulled the door open and stepped outside. He turned to get one last look at Mika before leaving. He pulled the door shut an inch at a time, careful to minimize the squeaking of the hinges and the click of the door latch.

Chris looked around for any signs of life but instead found an eerie quietness in the air. He was sure to find security guards wandering the property, so he made quick work to get inside the kitchen. He ran to the corner of each building, stopping to peer around the sides, and once clear, he continued on.

When he reached the entry to the dining hall where they were served dinner that very evening, he had no idea if the door would be locked or if he would have to break in. His plans lacked any sort of fine detail. Chris only knew what he wanted the end result to be. How exactly he would execute his master plan was completely up in the air.

He grabbed the doorknob, took a deep breath, and turned it as far as it would go. Success. With no clue what he would find inside, he thrust the door inward. The room was completely dark except for a faint, red light he could see through the double doors that led to the kitchen.

Chris stepped inside the dining hall and shut the door behind him. Rather than cut through the center room of tables in the dark, he chose instead to follow the outside circle to the right. Upon reaching the kitchen, he poked his head up to look through the glass of the right hand door. The kitchen was empty and lit only by a few red and green power-on lights from some of the appliances. He was close to getting what he needed and his heartbeat raced with anticipation.

He figured the first place to look was the back walk-in cooler. He believed a sneaky little tray exchange from dinner took place there, so it seemed the most obvious place to start. Chris walked over, grabbed the long silver handle, and pulled it, bringing the wide door open. The inside had a bright, white light and the crisp air gave him chills. He took a quick visual inventory but nothing seemed out of place. There were covered stainless steel pans, plastic crocks, and many boxes filled with various fruits, vegetables, eggs, and meat.

Unsure where to begin, Chris stepped completely into the cooler and closed the door behind him about ninety-five percent. He rifled through everything, one item at a time. One after another, the containers and boxes were dismissed as unhelpful. After sifting through everything he could see, Chris exhaled in frustration, rubbing the sweat from his forehead with his fingertips. When he removed his hand from his head, a small white box resting on the floor under a rack caught his eye. He was sure he didn't see it before. The box looked out of place, the only item actually on the floor, and in Chris' mind, a clear attempt to hide it.

"This looks promising," whispered Chris. The tiniest bit of hope rose in him as he grabbed the box. He cradled it with one arm against his chest and pulled the top open with the opposite hand. Inside sat three zip-top plastic bags with unknown dark matter. A little anxious, scared, and excited, he reached in and extracted one of the bags, guessing the weight to be about a pound, maybe a bit less.

When the contents hit the light, Chris knew instantly he was holding a human heart. Mixed emotions of validation and horror filled his mind, sending chills up his spine, and the realization that he just discovered a human organ in a kitchen cooler and the possible reasons it would be there, curdled his stomach.

"What the hell kind of place are they running here? This is unbelievable. What the hell did they bring us here for?" Chris just shook his head in disbelief and got back to his mission.

Evidence in hand, the time had come to get Mika and get out of there. He carelessly allowed the box to drop from his chest and rushed out of the cooler, stopping at the kitchen doors to peak through the glass once again. The room was still dark and the coast clear, so Chris burst through the doors and ran around the perimeter. When he reached the exterior door, he vigorously threw it open without checking for guards and burst from the dining hall in a straight line back to their room. After fifteen steps, he was startled by a voice coming from his right.

"Hey! Stop right there!" ordered one of the security guards from earlier.

His stride remained uninterrupted but Chris did glance over to see his pursuers. There were three of them this time. His heart beat quickened at the prospect of being chased, so he ran even faster. As he approached the now open door to their guest room, confusion overtook him. He wondered if Mika woke up and was looking for him. He actually hoped it was true. Not having to wake her was going to speed up their getaway.

From the doorway, he looked around the room, but Mika was nowhere in sight. "Mika, are you in here?" Chris shouted. "Mika!" He could see the bathroom door was open and the light off, so he assumed she had left. He whipped around to see if the guards had caught up and was blinded by the shine of a flash light directly into his eyes. He turned his head to escape it and saw the outline of three figures about twenty-five feet away. The one in the middle was obviously a woman, probably Brenda, though it seemed odd she would still be at the compound so late.

"Damn it, Mika. Where are you?" Chris said under his breath. With no intention of getting caught and his only thoughts to find Mika and show her the bag, he decided a delay tactic might work. "Hi. I thought I left my wallet in the dining room but I found it. No problem," Chris called out to the trio as he hid the bag behind his back.

The group crept forward, the woman standing slightly in front of the two men. As they stepped into the gleam of a parking lot light, Chris noticed something peculiar about the woman's face - there was duct tape over her mouth. Then he saw her eyes. It was Mika.

"You bastards! Let her go!" demanded Chris in an attempt to sound threatening, even though he knew they held all the power.

"You're not really in any position to be making demands. Are you, Mr. Quinn?" mocked the larger of the two security guards. "Drop whatever you have hiding behind your back and kindly step over here." The second guard pulled his hand clear from behind Mika's back to reveal a large knife. "So unless you want my cohort here to gut your woman, drop the fucking bag, right ... now." The guard's tone had turned intense and impatient.

Mika started to squirm but stopped when the blade poked her side, a reminder she was outmatched. Sure that Mika had learned her lesson, the guard mistakenly loosened his grip on her arm, and the second he did, Mika made a break for it, twisting past the outstretched arms of both guards and headed right at Chris. Before she even made it five steps, Mika suddenly stopped, threw her head up and arched her head back, obviously in pain. As she turned to the side, Chris could see the handle of the knife coming out of Mika's lower back. She turned back to Chris and tears filled her eyes when she caught the look of pale, white fear on his face. She suddenly dropped to her knees, then flat on the ground, face down, within a couple of seconds.

"Mika! Noooo!" yelled Chris. He dropped the bag but before he could step toward Mika, he felt a tap on his shoulder. He turned, expecting to see another guard, but to his surprise, the outline of a female stood before him. The woman reached to her left side and clicked the switch to turn the lights of the room on. Chris' mouth dropped open. It was Marsha Stonewall. Chris had no idea what to make of the situation. He could not fathom a single reason for her being there, let alone why his wife had just been stabbed and was lying dead in the parking lot.

Chris and Marsha just looked at each other in stark silence, as if each was waiting for the other to speak, or perhaps, no words were necessary. Just as Chris decided to say something, he detected something in Marsha's right hand. Without a word, Marsha drew her right hand to the neck of Chris, and with no vacillation, pressed and slid the chef's knife across his throat, severing his jugular.

Chris could do nothing but bring his hand to the wound in a failed effort to stop the bleeding. The crimson fluid poured and poured between his fingers and down his chest. He gurgled, trying to breathe, but choked on the blood, forcing him to spit some of it right on Marsha's face. She remained still and unfazed, watching with creepy satisfaction as Chris bled out. He finally collapsed to the ground, right at her feet.

The following evening, the final banquet of the weekend took place. Three couples sat around the table - The McFarlands, the Janikowskis, and the Browns. One chair remained empty. They all sipped wine and gossiped over the absence of Chris and Mika. When seven o'clock rolled around, the double doors from the kitchen opened and in walked Marsha Stonewall. Silence and awe instantly filled the room. She walked to the table and used the back of the one empty chair as a makeshift podium.

"Ladies and Gentlemen, I would like to thank you all for being here this weekend. As usual, this has been a very exciting and successful event." Marsha paused as the guests sitting around the large dining table clapped with enthusiasm. As the applause died down, Marsha continued, "Some years are rather ... monotonous, but this year's featured guests made for a very thrilling time. I had the pleasure of ... handling," Marsha made double quotes in the air with her fingers, "one of our generous benefactors myself this time around, and I must say how gratifying it will be to enjoy the taste of my own undertaking." The room erupted again with applause as everyone jumped to their feet. Marsha gently clapped along, nodding in acceptance.

Kitchen staff funneled through the double doors, their arms full of plates and bowls. They placed them on the table almost buffet style. The table guests continued their applause until all of the staff members had returned to the kitchen. Marsha inhaled deeply to enjoy all the exotic aromas from their soon to be devoured meal.

She signaled with her hands for everyone to settle and they all sat back down, again quiet and listening carefully. Still on her feet, she went on, "Please give thanks to our wonderful chefs for preparing this magnificent meal, and especially to Chris and Mikayla Quinn for providing us with the most decadent of ingredients for this feast." Marsha displayed a sinister grin as she pointed to an easel next to the table that held a large, white poster board. Glued on the surface was a picture of Chris and Mika standing in front of the compound's main office building, smiling wide and looking particularly happy. Also on the board, just above the image, were the words: This Year's Featured Guests - Chris and Mikayla Quinn.

"Now, let's eat."

DON'T MESS WITH THE BABYSITTER

FOREWORD:
While you read the following, dear reader, I encourage you to put on a pair of over-sized, counterfeit Dolce and Gabbana sunglasses, and perhaps, place a tiny Chihuahua in your Louis Vuitton handbag, as you play host to this bit of literary absurdity. Trust me, it will help. And don't be afraid to let the voice of our precious Brandy, be your voice as you channel the inner, modern day, valley girl residing in all of us.

O ... M ... G! I totally have to tell you what happened last week. It was the weirdest thing ever. It was like, in the paper and on the local news and everything. I mean, seriously, I'm like a celebrity at school now. The boys are totally checking me out more. Of course, I am pretty hot. I mean, look at me. All the girls, however, are like, way afraid of me, except for Hailey and Megan, my super besties.

Anyways, my next door neighbors, the Patterson's, rang my cellie on Friday after school, and they were like super desperate for a babysitter for their son Kaleb. He's four years old and really sweet. For once in my life, I had nothing to do, oddly enough, but I thought maybe I could get some homework done and watch Twilight for like, the bazillionth time, because Jacob is soooo hot, and I could watch him over and over and over again. Oh my god, I can't even hardly take it.

So, I agreed and showed up just before six that night, totally stoked to be gettin' some cheddar. I saw the most bad ass halter top at the mall a few weeks ago, and now ... I get ... to buy ... it. La lala lala la. Oh, that reminds me, I really need to catch up on Glee. I've been way busy lately, with like, self-defense classes and cheerleading practice and oodles of homework, so, like in desperation, I had to DVR like the last three episodes. It seriously pains me to not be able to discuss it with my besties, like really painful. Ok, Brandy, detour much? Sorry.

Anywho, I was needed at the Patterson's till like eleven or whatever, so after little Kaleb goes to bed, I'm just like sitting on the couch in their living room, and can I say, wicked nice place. The leather furniture is so Kardashian, I swear. And the seventy-inch flat screen, it's like I'm friends with Kim and Kourtney. But seriously, I was like halfway through Twilight, right where Edward and Bella ... oh, I'm sure you don't need me to tell you. I mean, really. Who hasn't seen it?

Well, just then, I heard something rattling at the back door in the kitchen. I admit ... I was a little S-P-A-Z-E-D, spazed out. Like, I totally almost tinkled in my pants and bit my tongue.

So, I paused the movie and just sat there ... listening. When I heard the glass break, I totally ... freaked. I swear, I must've like, hit my head on the ceiling I jumped so high. I quickly snatched my cellie off the table, but stupid me didn't plug it in when I got home, so like, the screen was black and totally dead. I thought for a second, phone, phone, phone. It's in the kitchen! Frick! But I figured, hey, I'm like super in shape and fast from cross country, so I'm going to run in there, grab the phone, and haul ass upstairs to call 9-1-1 and hide with Kaleb.

When I get to the doorway of the kitchen, I freeze when I see a hand reaching through the door to unlock it. I was so like, nervous and anxious, but really, I was like totally pissed at the audacity of these idiots. I mean, seriously, who robs a nice house in the 'burbs when there are like jewelry stores and Old Navy and pawnshops even. Think of all the frickin' cash, and gold chains and rockin' guitars in a pawnshop. Wicked good. Granted, it might be difficult to buy crack or prostitutes with a Gibson. Hmmm, now that I think about all the like, hassle to steal crap from people then have to sell it on craigslist or something. Oh, that is just way too much work.

It's totally like when my grandma buys me a hideous reindeer sweater from K-Mart, and I have to drag my butt to the east side of town to return the grotesque looking thing, only to get store credit. Store credit? The big, bad twenty-two year old college dropout manager can't give cash back without a receipt, apparently. Go back to your mom's basement. Loser! Uhhh! Then I like totally had to buy like a 20 pound bag of Twizzlers and a case of Vitamin Water with the store credit, because let's face it, I shouldn't even be in that place. You get the sitch. Way too much effort. Those jack-holes like totally need a better system.

Anyways, I have to admit, I kind of froze when I saw the hand. I know, not my finest moment, but it's not like I totally get robbed by amateurs every day. I stood there and watched the creepy, gloved hand pop the lock, then disappear back through the door. My heart about popped when the door slammed open. There were two guys standing there, looking quite ragged, with N-A-S-T-Y, naaaaaasty stained jeans, and absolutely stupid white hoodies. White? Really? It's like after Labor Day you idiots. Have some self-respect. Sooo frustrating.

At that point, I was just like, more annoyed than scared, and something inside of me just like kicked in. I was taking self-defense classes and I thought, maybe it was time to take out the trash. Take out the trash. That is too funny.

So, jackass number one said, "Hey little girl. Home all alone?" I said nothing, just give him a blank stare, which like, really confused him. He went on, "Hey! You hearing me you little bitch!" While he used his fingers to mimic sign language and tried to talk like a deaf person, idiot number one then said, "Are ... you ... here ... alone?" He turned to meth addict number two, both cracking up at their own ridiculous hilarity, which I found middle-schoolian, at best. I rolled my eyes so far back into my head, someone might have thought I was totally having a seizure.

Just then, I caught wind of their stench. Like totally revolted, I crinkled my nose and turned my head. Fowl beasts!

So I said, "Have you two, like ever ... taken a shower? Ugh! I think I might spew a strawberry Pop-tart all over this kitchen. What third world country's toilet did you just escape from? You are G-R-O-S-S, gross." They were not impressed with my defiance.

Loser number two pulled the front of his hoodie to his nose and took a big whiff. I rolled my eyes ... again. He then said, "Smells like winning to me you bitch." They laughed at their own exceptional wit. Quite disturbing.

So, moron number one takes a step forward and said, "Enough playing around! You got two choices. One, you can sit down in that chair while my friend here keeps an eye on you and I'll grab what we came here for. Or two, we can do this the hard way. And you don't wanna know what that entails. So what's it gonna be princess?"

I stood my ground, the courage like totally building inside me. Babysitters have a code you know. And the first and most important responsibility of even the worst of us is to protect the children, no ... matter ... what. I totally take that seriously. If anything ever happens to the little ones, you'll never sit again, totally black-listed. No way those crackheads were going to get me booted. So I got tough.

"Do NOT ... come any closer to me loser!" I like, put my index finger up, just to make sure he knew I was way serious and then I said, "I mean it. There will be trouble." I couldn't even believe how calm and assertive I was. I'm pretty sure the self-defense classes were paying off.

So, drug monkey number one said, "Ooo ... what's a little girl like you gonna do, like totally," the wanker flipped his hair, "kick my ass?" He was obviously mocking me, but I never flip my hair like that. Rude. Of course, both shameless degenerates laughed out loud, again drastically overestimating their way bad senses of humor.

I put up both my hands, fingers extended, "Freaks! I'm not screwing around here. Please take that ... homeless guy funk and really bad fashion sense back out that door, and we'll totally pretend this never happened. I won't even call the police or anything."

Just then, momma's boy number one gave a signal to stoner number two to come at me, and he immediately like, ran up on me. Two things popped into my head. First, I knew I had to do something or else that loser was going to put his grubby, filthy little hands on me. Ick! Second, my inner babysitting lioness that only wanted to protect my little cub, just totally, all out, kicked in and surprised the crap out of stupid-ass number two by stiff-arming him right in the middle of his gnarly and vulgarly disgusting chest. Before he even knew what hit him, I totally slapped him stone cold right in the face with my other hand. He stumbled back and I totally seized the opportunity to grab his arm, and like totally judo flipped him. I'm not kidding, like serious superhero stuff here. It was so bad-ass I almost couldn't deal. And I totally heard a bone crack, like way loud when his shoulder and head smacked into the floor. Douche bag number one and I both totally cringed at the sound. It was way gruesome.

So, with mental patient number two on the ground, like totally knocked out, I lay a way sinister gaze on upchuck number one. I was breathing pretty heavy at that point, my chest and nostrils puffing like a bull about to give someone a serious horn throttling. I'm not sure what was going through the other turd's mind, but he totally looked like he didn't know whether to crap himself or cry.

I guess he made his choice when he started to scream like a banshee and bolted right at me. In the blink of an eye, he totally entered my quadrant and like, without a thought, I placed a forward kick as hard as I could right at, well ... let's face it, his most certainly diseased and infested crotch. He lost all his forward momentum, and in fact, his feet came about six inches off the ground from the force of my way intense, totally bad-ass kick.

Inbred number one grabbed his 'private and should never be touched by anyone area' with both hands and fell straight on his knees, totally moaning in pain. Idiot. What did he think I was going to do? Just like, stand there and get whooped? Hells no! That low-life was going down. So, like really on fire, I launched the final blow and totally cold-cocked that mindless meth head right in his grill, knocking him flat on his back, out like a light.

I didn't even have time to admire my work because just as the filth hit the floor, I heard a whimper from behind me. I turned to see little Kaleb standing not far away but still in the living room, totally shocked at what he had just witnessed. I turned to him and told him everything was ok. That little cutie was super scared, so he ran over and gave me a big hug, with a tiny tear coming down his cheek. I just about lost it.

I released Kaleb but kept him close. I quickly grabbed the phone and called the police. They arrived way fast and I told them the whole story while they arrested and hauled away the trash boys. They could hardly believe how I totally took care of business. I think the nervousness finally settled in, because after just a few minutes of talking to me, they kept having to tell me to slow down as I told them what happened. They said I was in shock or something, but no way. I was just talking a mile a minute, like always. Like right now. OMG. How funny is that?

And of course, the cops called the Patterson's, who then came home early, which I was totally bummed about. Obviously, I had everything under control, but oh well. They were so like, terrified about the ordeal but super-stoked that Kaleb and I were safe and nothing was stolen. Only the backdoor had to be repaired, and that was like, not a big deal, so said Mr. Patterson. They were so extremely grateful and appreciative of my heroism, they paid me five Benjamins. Holy crap! I totally smelled a shopping spree. So excited!

I know one thing, my babysitting resume got way, like super-charged. Everyone talked about it and still talk about what happened. My client list like totally increased, so much so, I couldn't possibly take every opportunity, which way blows because I could use the money. This brings up an interesting idea. I really think I should charge more for my services, because let's face it, in my neighborhood, you don't mess with the babysitter, and that has totally got to be worth something.

THEY SMELL THE DEAD

The sky is black, morphing into crimson as it flows to the horizon. Bands of clouds gray the view and mask the stars. The landscape is almost sinister but somehow beautiful. In the distance, I see the tiniest of specks, dynamic and moving like a single organism. I squint in a poor attempt to distinguish the now growing mass. I realize they are getting closer and closer but no matter how much I want to, I cannot move my feet.

I stare helplessly when suddenly I know what they are. Birds. Several dozen, maybe even close to a hundred, it is hard to be sure. As they grow near, I can see their wingspans are enormous and I panic a little. The birds are coming right for me, no longer in the sky above but maybe ten feet off the ground and coming fast. As they pass a series of street lights at the end of the block, I see the heads of a few. These damn things are vultures.

I have never once seen a kettle of vultures fly like this - a freight train with no brakes. I still can't move my feet. Shit, shit, shit, I think. What the hell am I going to do? If they don't see me and we collide, I'm done for.

I look around, desperate for a solution but I see no one or anything that can help me. With no other choice, I quickly crouch down to help minimize the exposure, wrapping my arms around my knees as I press my face to my legs. A few seconds go by but I don't hear anything. I pull my head up to see if perhaps they have pulled up and flown by. I slowly open my right eye and scream as a vulture careens toward my face.

I yell as I violently jerk back against my pillow, safe and sound in my bed. I've never been so happy in my life to see the beautifully textured ceiling of my bedroom.

Holy crap. I feel relief and let out a big sigh. I try to catch my breath and bring my mind back down to reality. I've always found it weird how when you first come out of a nightmare, the dream world and the real one blur together in a confusing left brain-right brain battle. A few minutes pass and I am finally calm as the dream fades and almost disappears from memory.

I suppose I shouldn't be surprised by this type of dream. I am very sick. I have barely left the bed in months. I have the strength to get to the bathroom and back, but that is about it these days. Cancer is an unrelenting son of a bitch. For years and years it grew in my system, spread itself around a little, and finally caused the slightest pain in my abdomen. By then it was way too late. The cancer had spread to multiple organs, to my lymphatic system, and into my bones - aggressive, to say the least. I didn't bother with treatment. My chance of surviving six months either way was less than one percent. I opted for being one kind of sick instead of two.

To be honest, no one should feel sorry for me. I deserve to die. I have done a whole lot of really bad things in my life. The way I see it, the cancer is the Universe's way of getting even. I have never believed in karma but it sure is hard to deny the irony. I don't care to share the intimate details of my many transgressions, but suffice it to say, my actions have ruined the lives of many people.

My heart nearly jumps from my chest at the sound of three rhythmic and forceful taps on my bedroom window. This is unusual at any time of day, but at 3 a.m., I am particularly alarmed. I sit quietly for a minute and listen, my pulse still racing. I can't help but think I am hearing things, perhaps still drifting in and out of the dream state.

I calm down some and start to feel a little more awake when I hear the taps again. Maybe it's a tree branch but I don't think there are any trees that close to my doors or windows. Besides, the pattern sounds deliberate. I am sure as hell not expecting any visitors, and even if I was, I would tell the person where the key was hidden outside before they came, since it's very difficult for me to answer the door on most days.

The noise is going to drive me nuts if I don't figure out what it is, and more importantly, how to get rid of it. I will myself to my feet, and slightly hunched over, stumble with heavy steps to the window. I stand there for a few minutes, winded and trying to gather the strength to open the shade. I really need my oxygen. Damn it. It's over by the bed. I have no choice but to just deal with my circumstance. I give myself a quick pep talk, then reach forward with both arms and throw open the curtains. They are much heavier than I remember.

A beady, yellow eye just two inches from the glass stares back, scaring the crap out of me. I let out a yelp and stumble backward until I hit the bed, falling right onto it. I lay there for a few seconds, terrified to check the window again. I am sure it is just a dream.

When my childish fear finally subsides, I turn to the left to help push my body up. With only my eyes, I glance to the window and see nothing but pitch dark. I let out a huge sigh of relief and note how big my imagination is. I wonder if my pain meds need to be adjusted. Apparently, I'm hallucinating. My morphine is pretty much the end of the line for pain management and there is no way in hell I can take less, so I doubt there is anything that can be done.

I scoot down the bed and grab the oxygen mask, put it to my face, and press the button. Ah ... sweet, relaxing gas. With each inhale, my lungs and heart calm a bit, my nerves as well. I peek to the window again knowing I can't very well leave the curtain open all night, so I decide to make another trip over.

Before I can even put the mask down, I start to hear an odd tapping from the ceiling. More hallucinations? It seems pretty damn real. It begins in a single location toward the corner of the room near the window, but multiplies over and over again until finally reaching an ear-splitting crescendo of scratching and knocking. An instant headache takes hold. I decide not to even screw around with it.

I drop the oxygen and pick up my cell phone from the nightstand. I press and hold my lucky number three, which auto dials my hospice company's 24-hour care line. It rings three times before someone answers.

"Hello, Mr. Henderson. This is Naomi. Is everything ok?"

"Well, I have a really bad headache and I've kind of been hearing strange noises." My voice is elevated in a futile attempt to overcome the noise from my room. I hold back the part about a vulture staring me down through the bedroom window. I want to ease her into my nightmare.

"I can hear you just fine, Mr. Henderson. No need to yell. Have you taken anything for the headache?" She conveniently ignores the second half of my confession.

"I'm on the morphine but other than that, no." The noises suddenly and completely die out. I pause and look to the ceiling, listening. I repeat what I had said about the morphine but at a normal volume, then I decide to take the plunge and just get right to it. "I think I may need an adjustment to the meds or something. I've been, well ... seeing and hearing things tonight, things I know could not possibly be there. I just wanted to check in and see if this is normal and if there is anything that can be done."

"Hallucinations are a side effect of the morphine. Perhaps we can adjust the dosage. And I would go ahead and take a couple of extra strength acetaminophen tablets for the headache. Are you experiencing any other symptoms?"

I think about her question for a moment. "No. Everything is fine otherwise."

"Ok, Mr. Henderson. We'll send somebody out right away to adjust the meds and just check in on you, make sure you're all right. It will take about thirty minutes to get there. Will you be ok until someone arrives or should I call an ambulance?"

"Oh yeah, I'll be fine. I'll just stay in bed to be on the safe side." I am much calmer just speaking to another human being and feeling better already. "Thank you." We exchange goodbyes and I close the phone before sitting it back on the nightstand.

I sit for a moment, just trying to breathe as deeply as I can, which isn't much to speak of. The throbbing in my head has mostly subsided but I am utterly spent energy wise. My arms and legs feel like they are encased in concrete. I look to the window again and decide the nurse can draw the curtains for me when she arrives. There is no way I can make it over there again, not without ending up on the floor.

With all the strength I can muster, I turn my body parallel to the bed and carefully, nearly in slow-motion, pull my legs up, dragging them against the edge of the mattress. Once I am sure I'm in a comfortable position, I release the tension from my back muscles and plop back onto my pillow. I lay perfectly still with my eyes closed for what seems like hours. In reality, only four minutes pass.

Just as my eyes ride the edge of being too heavy to keep open, I am startled awake by the sound of glass breaking somewhere in the house. I stay still, looking at the ceiling and hoping I have just imagined the noise. I have no such luck. I can hear glass scattering about on the floor of the kitchen, the only tiled area of the home where this can be possible, and I hear an odd shuffling sound. Then the tapping on the ceiling starts up again.

I hear a thud as something makes contact with my bedroom window and I about jump out of my skin. The adrenaline brings me up in bed and I quickly look in the direction of the window. I notice the tiniest glint in the middle of the glass. It has broken from the impact. Out of the darkness comes a vulture making another impact in the exact same spot, causing a spider-web pattern to instantly appear across the entire pane, crackling at each step and moving outward from the center.

Why are these goddamned birds trying to get into my house? Come on hospice! When are you going to get here?

I have no clue what to do next. I do realize if that vulture smashes into the window one more time, it will surely give way and I will have a big, black feathered mess on my hands. Suddenly, it dawns on me that the only location within the house that does not have a window is the bathroom. If I can somehow make it in there, I will be safe until the nurse arrives, and perhaps he or she can call an exterminator or animal control or whomever deals with odd bird invasions. The Hitchcock movie comes to mind. Poor Tippie getting her golden locks plucked from her head is not the image I need at this moment. I currently have no hair on my head, as I keep it shaved, but I can think of other things they might jab at. No thank you.

Without even really knowing if I can make it, I grab my phone, twist around to the side of the bed, and slowly slide off the edge until my feet hit the ground. My bathroom door is about fifteen feet away and I am confident I can make it. One baby step at a time, I nervously and groggily make my way toward safety. My headache has returned on account of the ear-numbing tapping and clawing, and I am pretty sure the rest of the house is filled with vultures by this point too, so I have no choice but to ignore the head pain and push on.

When I reach the doorway of the bathroom, I take a guarded look out of the bedroom door and into the hallway. I lose my breath when I see a dozen or more sets of beady, yellow eyes looking right at me. The vultures have seized control of the house. For the life of me I can't figure out why on Earth they want to be in here so bad. The only idea I can muster is perhaps a possum, a cat, or a raccoon has gotten in the house and died somewhere this evening, and the vultures are picking up on it. This doesn't really explain the weird dream about them, but hey, I am on death's door, riddled with cancer, and pumped full of brain fogging medications. Considering all of that, the dream isn't really all that bizarre.

When the vultures from the hallway start to get closer, I decide it is time to lock myself in the sanctuary of the master bath, so I reach in and flick on the light, and just before I take my first step inward, the third impact I feared with the vulture from outside comes. A burst of thick pieces of glass shoot into the room leaving no corner untouched. Instinctually, I turn, drop to my knees, and cover my face to avoid being hit by debris. Very little glass actually hits me, and the pieces that do are tiny enough that they do not cut me.

The scavenging intruder loses control of its flight and smacks sideways right into the side of the bed where I had just been sitting not two minutes before. Good thing I moved my ass to the bathroom.

My theory about an animal being dead in the house is quickly dismissed as I discover the vultures are actually closing in on me, quite deliberately. The first group from the hall reaches the bedroom doorway. When they see the much larger vulture that just crashed through my bedroom window get to its feet and look their way, they stop advancing, almost as if they have been given a signal to stand down. I guess I know who the Alpha bird is.

The boss vulture shakes its head to help regain its bearings and then sets its gaze for me. I scramble away from the door, trying to clear a path so that I can shut it, but I am not fast enough. The vulture spreads its wings and uses them for balance as it hops to the bathroom in three large leaps.

I lean forward and place one hand around the door just as the bird sinks the end of its beak into my right leg, just above my ankle. I scream in pain but still manage to hold onto the door, which I immediately try to slam shut. My leg is in the way, so the door catches on my foot and does not make impact with the vulture as I hoped. The damn thing does not release its grip. Instead, it sinks its beak deeper, causing me to wince and holler again. I release the door as my attacker uses its entire and surprisingly high amount of strength to pull me out of the bathroom. I'm most of the way out before I can grab the door jamb, but it's no use, my fingers slip as I am just too weak to resist.

The other vultures are bouncing and chirping in anticipation of my capture and I can only assume I am their next meal. I finally run completely out of energy and fall to my back as I am dragged across the bedroom floor. When we get to the group, the boss releases its beak and jumps over the crowd of vultures, taking flight right into the foyer. Without hesitating, it flies right into the front door, smashing it to bits, then keeps on going, never to return.

The rest of the melee members seem less controlled and much more demonic. They dance and squawk and peck like a rowdy mosh pit. All at once, they descend upon me, grabbing anywhere they can, and holding tight. The pain is unbearable and I nearly pass out from all the punctures. If it wasn't for the morphine, I doubt I could still be conscious.

Like a well-oiled machine, they all move in unison by pulling my body along the floor, through the house, and out the front doorway. I do not resist. What is the point? I have no strength left and I am probably nearing the last days of my fight with cancer, which let's face it, isn't really much of a fight. I resign to my fate and allow the birds to take me unchallenged.

Once out on the lawn, the birds release me and some fly away into the night sky. The four that stay, the largest of the group, reposition themselves around me and once again take hold of me, this time by jumping on my body and sinking their talons in deep. Lined up in a perfect row not unlike a bobsled team, they begin flapping their enormous wings and we lift off the ground. I notice the sky is black and filled with stars now. The clouds have moved on. I take pleasure in the beauty of the night sky as we fly closer to the stars and further away from my home.

Eventually, the air seems to grow too thin to breathe and I start to suffocate. I writhe and gasp but the vultures keep flying higher and higher. It takes about two minutes for the job to be done. My carriers never once flinch and never once stop climbing. Finally, my heart stops. With no life left, I become the blackness.

A NEIGHBORLY SCOURGE

Love thy neighbor - but don't pull down your hedge.
Benjamin Franklin

I live in a diverse and spectacular middle class neighborhood. The yards and bushes are well manicured, the trees are mature, and the houses are a good mix of shapes, sizes, and textures. Aside from the pleasant and peaceful charm of Locust Street, the people that live here are its greatest asset. The unique personalities, the growing families, and the jumble of generations all work to make my street a great place to spend my retirement years.

I enjoy many hours just sitting in my living room recliner watching and listening to the sights and sounds of life here. Two school buses pass each morning around eight and again just after three-thirty. Children on bikes zoom by, people meander down the sidewalk, some pulled by their dogs, joggers sweat through their outfits, and teenagers cruise down the block, windows and steel rattling from the overused bass.

About a year ago, a nice, young couple with a pre-school age boy moved in across the street. Tom, Cynthia, and Jacob McCarron were friendly and involved. They hosted a cookout for the neighborhood shortly after moving in, and everyone had a great time getting to know them, drinking some beer and enjoying the delicious potluck dishes. The family was quickly accepted and within a few short weeks it was like they had always been here.

Six weeks after the McCarrons arrived, their neighbors on the right hand side from my view, the Johnsons, suddenly left the neighborhood without a word. They told no one they were leaving, and not a single person witnessed them pack and move. They were just gone. A for-sale sign was put in the yard and twenty-four hours later it was marked sold. Considering the number of hours I spend just watching the street from my chair, I found it odd that I never once saw an actual person coming or going from that house during the week they had supposedly moved. I didn't even see a real estate agent or potential buyers. With no warning, the Johnsons were gone, the house was put on the market and sold, and a new family had moved in. Odd.

Compared to the McCarron's delightful entry into the neighborhood, the Smith family arrived with much less fanfare. From the second their U-Haul truck entered the driveway, a general sense of malaise took over the entire block. Patrick Smith completely avoided chatting with anyone. Susie, his wife, and Matthew, their four year old son, were a little friendlier but still kept mostly to themselves. The strangest thing of all was how the Smiths and McCarrons interacted. More accurately, I suppose, was their near complete lack of interaction. They barely acknowledged each other's existence. They would mow their respective yards on opposite days and even left their houses a few minutes apart to avoid driveway mingling. There was no talking, no friendly waves, and no eye contact. In addition to this behavior, the McCarrons became more withdrawn, mirroring the conduct of the newly arrived Smith family.

The strange nature of their relationship, if you can call it that, came to a head two months after the Smith's arrival. On a beautiful, Spring Saturday in early May, something rare happened. In a case of strange coincidence, or perhaps it was something more, the wives and children of the McCarron and Smith homes were gone for the day, and much to my surprise, both Tom McCarron and Patrick Smith worked on the landscaping in their yards simultaneously.

Neither man acknowledged the presence of the other. Lawns were mowed, hedges trimmed, and sidewalks swept. To my amazement, the men did not exchange a single glance in over an hour of being not more than one hundred feet from each other. I had no choice but to stay glued to my chair, peering out the window like a rubbernecking driver passing an automobile accident. I could not take my eyes away out of sheer, morbid curiosity. I was sure it would be impossible for them to avoid each other forever and I couldn't help but wonder why they acted in such fashion. If they had known each other before they moved to the neighborhood and had a problem with each other, I doubt the Smiths would have bought the home directly next door. There was definitely something peculiar going on, and May 18th, at five minutes after eleven in the a.m., would be the day the truth was revealed.

Patrick Smith stood in his driveway, long clippers in hand, glaring at the low hanging branches from his neighbor's tree that happened to be invading his property. Every time his wife pulled the minivan down the drive, the twigs and leaves scrapped the top of her vehicle, and Patrick was determined to do something about it. Little did Patrick know, but Tom McCarron was busy pushing a broom along his front sidewalk, all the while paying close attention to the movements of the green-handled tree trimmers held at Patrick's side.

Tom, in a matter of fact sort of way, pushed and walked, pushed and walked, until he hit the edge of the Smith driveway. He pretended to look at the debris in front of his broom while peeking over repeatedly at Patrick, who studied the branches of the tree overhanging his driveway.

Patrick had no intention of annihilating the tree. He just wanted it trimmed in such a way that would keep the branches above the six foot tall fence, thus preventing them from scratching his vehicles. He quickly identified the culprits and made fast work of cutting at seven spots, allowing each collection of twigs and leaves to fall to the driveway, all of which he intended to chop down even further and set out to the curb.

His neighbor Tom, owner of the tree, continued his charade of sweeping and watching until he noticed the manner in which Patrick was cutting the branches. There was a technique to trimming trees to avoid disease. This involved clean, angled cuts made a few inches from the connection point. Tom nearly jumped out of his skin in disgust as he witnessed the dull blades of Patrick's rusty tool carelessly hacking and gnawing at the tree, leaving frayed and damaged ends much too close to the surviving branches. Tom threw his broom down to the sidewalk and marched over to Patrick, no longer able to contain his rage.

By that point, I had moved from my spot in the living room to the swing on my front porch. Nosy Nelly that I am, I just had to hear the details.

"Excuse me sir! What exactly do you think you're doing to my tree?" asked Tom, stopping about three feet from Patrick.

Startled by the presence of Tom, not having seen him approach, Patrick jumped back a little but didn't say anything. He was so deep in the thought of his work, he needed a few moments to process the words he heard. Tom grew impatient.

"Well? Care to explain what you're doing there?" asked Tom.

Puzzled by the intrusion, Patrick finally answered, "I'm uh ... trimming the branches of this tree. They're hanging too low and keep scratching my cars. It's no problem. I think I got it. Thank goodness for gardening tools." Patrick held up the trimmers and seemed completely oblivious to Tom's tone. This only appeared to infuriate Tom that much more.

"Well, there is a right and a wrong way to do that." Tom snatched the tool from Patrick's hand. "And these things are so dull, it's a wonder they cut anything at all. You may have just killed my tree!"

"Pardon me? How rude! Give those back!" Patrick lunged to grab the tool but Tom stepped back to avoid the move.

"No way. I'm not going to let you further destroy my tree." Tom stopped for a second to think about his next move. Only a few moments passed before he decided. He turned to the street and launched the clippers high into the air toward the end of the driveway. When they landed just into the road, the green plastic handles exploded off, separating from the blades, never to be used again for their intended purpose.

Patrick stood in amazement at the audacity of his neighbor, completely unsure how to react. When Tom turned back to him, Patrick finally responded, "You son of a bitch. What the hell is your problem?" They looked each other right in the eyes, the gears of barbarism turning in both men.

I sat slack jawed at the developments. As far as anyone knew, these guys didn't even know each other, yet there they were, tussling like old, mortal enemies.

"That's a beautiful, old tree and you're hacking it up," said Tom.

"I don't see a problem here. I had to do what I thought was necessary to protect my property. And you destroyed my tool. You'll have to replace that." Patrick pointed to the street as he made his demand.

"Oh ... I don't think so. Unless you have a time machine and can go back and not slice and dice my tree all to hell, then those clippers are finished, and I will not be responsible for putting a second set in your hands so you can do more damage." Tom was fed up, so he turned and walked down the driveway to pick up his broom and headed home.

At first, Patrick just stood by and watched. He finally gave in to his rage and ran down the drive and into the street where the clipper blades laid. He picked them up and ran past Tom to the convertible sitting in Tom's driveway. Patrick turned to face his neighbor, holding the tip of the blades near the door, close to the passenger side mirror, ready to act.

Tom stopped at the end of his own driveway, about fifteen feet from the rear of his beloved car. "Just what in the hell are you doing? Don't you dare touch my car," said

Tom, shaking his head in disapproval. "Don't ... you ... do it."

"Apologize and promise to replace these, and I'll walk away. Otherwise, the bitch gets it." Malice dripped from Patrick's lips.

"I will not apologize and you wouldn't dare."

"I guess you don't know me very well, Mr. McCarron." With an unwavering stare at Tom, Patrick pressed the end of the blades to the car and slowly took the edge down the length of the door, stopping at the seam.

The noise made the hair on the back of my neck stand straight up, even all the way across the street.

"Oops. Looks like you got a little scratch there." Patrick looked at his handy work and pursed his lips. "Oh, that looks really bad."

"You heartless bastard! How could you?" The tension in Tom's voice suggested a much more heinous act had occurred, as if Patrick had kidnapped Tom's son and not simply damaged his car, so it became clear how much he loved the vehicle. "I've had just about enough of this."

Tom once again threw his broom to the ground and instead grabbed the gas-powered hedge trimmers sitting in his yard about three feet away. He bolted back to Patrick's property, pulling the cord to start the motor as he walked over to the bushes lining the front of his neighbor's house. He made quick work by randomly and haphazardly cutting through them in waves of ecstasy as he evened the score. The damage done was severe and traumatizing enough to the boxwoods that they would never recover, replacement the only option.

"Oh, that is just wonderful," said Patrick, throwing his hands in the air in disgust. "Well, maybe you'll understand this." He walked over to Tom's car, hopped onto the hood, unzipped his pants, and proceeded to urinate on the windshield, purposefully arcing every few seconds to squirt a little on the dash and the front seats.

When Tom came around the edge of the fence and caught sight of Patrick's vulgar display, I could tell something inside of him just snapped. The battle had just become more than a figurative and quite literal pissing contest - it became a war. And as if not bewildering enough, the most bizarre occurrences I had ever witnessed began to happen, unexplainable things, magical things.

As Patrick finished his business, Tom stood very still with his hands together and out in front of him, only the corresponding fingertips touching each other. His gaze locked on Patrick, who stayed on top of the car, looking as puzzled as I was. Slowly, Tom drew his hands apart until he extended them just past shoulder width, then he thrust his hands and arms forward in the direction of Patrick. Some mysterious force transferred from his palms and hit Patrick, sending him flying backward off the hood of the car and onto the ground about ten feet away.

I kept closing and rubbing my eyes, trying to understand what I had just witnessed, wondering if perhaps I was actually asleep and dreaming. But what I saw that day was real, it was just that my mind had trouble processing the event. I sat glued, mouth agape, and eyes fixed on the two men across the street as they continued with no end in sight.

Patrick, a little dazed from the impact of the invisible force, or from hitting the ground, or both, slowly got to his feet while shaking his head in an effort to reestablish his equilibrium. He dusted himself off and casually put away his weapon, buttoning and zipping his pants.

Tom was breathing heavily, as if he had just run up a hillside. He was bent over with his hands on his knees and didn't notice Patrick get up from the ground. At about the same time, both men gathered themselves enough to stare each other down once again, but now it was Patrick's turn in this 'monkey see, monkey do' battle for neighborly respect.

Patrick walked calmly back over to the vehicle, ready to give it one last taste of vengeance. He placed the palms of his hands down on the hood, and similarly to how Tom had earlier, seemed to garner a hidden power within, using his hands to focus an unseen energy. His hands trembled as electricity sparked in the microscopic space between his fingertips and the car. A soft, blue light reflected off the car. Tom had no idea what Patrick was planning to do, he just stood by and watched, fire building in his own belly.

Just as the energy made a barely audible hum in the air, a sudden surge of power escaped Patrick's hands, releasing into the convertible with a loud thud that I could feel all the way across the street. Two seconds later, all four tires simultaneously exploded, sending shredded rubber like you often see on the highway, across the yard, into the street, and against the house. Another moment later, the metal underside of the car crunched to the concrete driveway, no longer elevated by the tires. Scratched, dented, peed on, and without wheels, the once beautiful car now looked like it belonged in the junkyard or parked next to a trailer-home somewhere near the edge of town. Either way, Tom was not pleased.

And just as I thought about how amazing it was they had not drawn the attention of other people, Tom's other neighbor, Todd Whitehurst, a man in his mid-forties who often worked from home doing some kind of insurance claims, came marching outside to see what caused the loud explosion. If I hadn't seen the actual events for myself, I would have guessed by the sound that an electrical transformer had blown somewhere on the block.

Todd walked to the middle of his own yard and paused briefly before turning to his left where he noticed the mangled vehicle. He knew it didn't usually look like a wreck. He then saw Patrick and Tom standing at opposite ends of Tom's driveway. He had no idea what had just happened and wanted to make sure no one was hurt, so he hustled across his own yard and into Tom's, getting about halfway before speaking up. By that point, Patrick and Tom were boiling with rage, and they looked ready to rip each other apart.

"What the hell happened out here?" asked Todd in a serious, yet concerned tone.

Neither man had any tolerance at that moment for any interruption in their feud, and almost as if they had scripted it, both turned to Todd, Patrick's eyes glowing icy blue and Tom's burning fire red, and growled in sync, "Don't worry about it!"

Todd turned stark white, and though I am not one hundred percent sure, may have wet himself. Without another word, he turned and ran horrified back to his house, slamming the front door behind him. I sat mesmerized by what I had witnessed, and quite frankly, a little terrified of what might happen next, and more to the point, what they might do to me if they caught on to my presence. With no regard for my own safety, I continued on, and so did they.

Tom and Patrick looked back to each other, giving an unspoken acknowledgement of their surprising unity in dispatching Todd. The camaraderie passed as quickly as it arrived and the battle ensued like no interruption had even taken place.

Tom turned his head up and to the right, thinking briefly about his next move when an idea sprouted. The garage. Tom hustled over to the end of Patrick's drive, setting his sights on the detached two-car garage just behind the house. Patrick quickly followed to the sidewalk, stopping to watch Tom's next move for a second before starting to conjure his own spell.

Tom put a hand in the air, index finger pointing straight up. He started twirling the finger in small circles, slowly at first, then faster and faster and faster, until at last, he threw his hand in the direction of the garage. A fury of tornado like winds surged, one after another toward the structure in continual gusts. Each impact was harder than the one before, shaking the garage until finally pushing the structure backward ten feet off the foundation. The entire upper half fell slightly out of kilter, cracking into a staircase shaped line from the left edge to the peak. With the final blast, the roof of the garage became completely detached, and with nothing holding it on, it slid right off, crashing into the ground and the backyard fence.

Patrick barely noticed, busy with his own incantation. He stood still, focusing on the front of Tom's house. With his left hand out in front of him, he opened and closed his hand rhythmically like a ticking clock. All the oxygen seemed to leave the air for a moment, and when Patrick felt that change, he left his hand closed for five seconds before thrusting his fingers open wide, holding them there as a sonic boom burst across the yard, tossing the dilapidated car over. The pulse also hit the house and with such force that it shattered every window. The house did remain standing, unlike the garage next door, which had seen better days.

Tom heard the crunch of his car smashing to the ground and the glass shattering, instantly wiping the grin from his face. He bolted back to his own yard to see the damage. He now seemed less concerned about the car and more worried about his house.

"It's one thing to wreck a man's car, but you ... you ... hit my house. Not cool man. You just brought this fight to another level ... neighbor," Tom finished with snarky disdain. Tom officially lost his mind and marched right back over to Patrick's house, standing on the sidewalk near the street, purposely keeping himself at a distance from the house. Patrick stayed behind, more concerned with deciding his own game plan. I had a bad feeling about Tom's next possible move. The fire in his eyes revealed all.

He stood with his head bowed, his arms at his side, and palms facing out toward the house. I could see his thumbs shaking as his hands gradually turned from white to pink to red hot. The smell of the air changed like someone had lit a fireplace.

When Patrick noticed the odor, it broke his train of thought. He quickly ran to his yard, arriving just in time to see Tom bring his arms above his head, then thrust his hands at the house, sending two streams of quite beautiful orange, yellow, and crimson fire at the home.

The molten energy pierced the house instantly, setting the siding and the front door on fire. The blaze caught so fast, the heat so intense, it was only a matter of seconds before the entire two-story was engulfed in a roaring inferno.

Patrick stood paralyzed. I could tell he was debating whether he should run in and attempt to save any of his belongings, but it was way too late for that. The heat and flames were so intense, the glass started to break, the structure rocked and began collapsing, and the roof caved within two minutes.

Both men just watched the home burn, never once even looking at one another. Tom instantly realized the impact of what he had done and regretted it. Patrick fell to his knees in shock, all the enthusiasm he once held for their battle completely exhausted.

Personally, I decided it was time to get more involved myself, so I stealthily got up and moved to enter the house to call the fire department, just in case no one else in the neighborhood had by then. When I reached the front door, I turned to get another look across the street when I noticed a small line of flames on the ground, running between the two houses near the wreckage of what was once Patrick's garage. A cable or wire that ran from one property over to the other had caught fire and was bound for Tom's house. I surmised that the potential this fire now had to do even more damage was high, so I rushed in and made the call. When I returned to the porch, I remained still as I witnessed both houses burning, Tom's catching up fast to Patrick's already burned out shell of a home.

Tom had made his way over to watch his own house burn down, helpless to do anything. Eventually, both men could look no more, so they sat on the curb, facing my house, each near the end of their respective driveways. Their homes now consisted mostly of cinder, flame, rubble, ash, and soot. The only untouched thing from their joint destruction was the massive tree on the property line, the one responsible for their initial argument. When they realized this fact, they joined each other in a hardy laugh. They both had lost the battle, and instead, the tree had won. They acknowledged the ridiculous nature of their fight, and for the first time, actually physically touched by shaking hands and agreeing to never let anything like that happen again. The mysterious power they both seemed to possess was too great to allow for further bickering that might end in someone really getting hurt, and they didn't want that.

By the time the fire department arrived, it was too late to save either house, but they did extinguish the flames so that no other homes would get involved. When asked about the circumstances that caused the fire, neither man had any answers. They just shook their heads in an unspoken, unifying denial of circumstance. The investigation would later reveal the fire was started by an unexplained phenomenon, which as far as I was concerned, was completely true. Only the three of us knew the truth, and I only tell the truth of what I saw that day now because I believe enough time has passed that no one would believe me anyway. Call it an urban legend, the musings of a crazy old lady from the neighborhood, or a good fireside story to tell at camp. It doesn't really matter. I'll always know what I saw, and it defies believability, even for me, but it did happen.

The neighborhood buzzed for months, the gossip rampant. Even as the lots were cleared and new homes constructed by the McCarron and Smith families, theories were abound with no hypothesis even close to the reality of that day. I often played along, giving strange ideas that were purposefully misleading, just to feel like a part of the neighborhood and not seem like a prude.

The two new houses turned out wonderful and are great additions to an already charming neighborhood. Tom and Patrick became good friends, their families spending a lot of time together too. Their sons, Jacob and Matthew, both being around the same age, became fast friends as well, and they were often seen playing together in one or both of the two yards, or up and down the sidewalk, always within yelling distance of their parents.

Today, I sit on my front porch on a beautiful Saturday afternoon, drinking some iced tea and watching the usual neighborhood rousing's. Jacob McCarron and Matthew Smith run up and down the Smith driveway, chasing each other playing tag. On one of the trips down the drive, Jacob spots something on the curb just across the street, right in front of the house next door to me.

The boys stop running after Jacob points to the item. They have a quick discussion about it and without warning, run full speed across the street without looking for traffic. Luckily, no cars are present, allowing them safe passage.

When they reach the item, a recently discarded but perfectly functioning red Wiffle ball bat, each boy places a hand on it but each stops short for a moment of attempting to pick it up. They look right into each other's eyes.

"It's mine," demands Jacob.

"No way! I touched it first," proclaims Matthew.

"But I'm the one who saw it first, so hands off," says Jacob.

Just then, the bat lifts into the air, each boy with one hand near it, but neither actually touching it. Without another word, the gaze they exchange somehow turns different, more sinister than a simple 'boys being boys' type aggression. I cannot believe what I see as Jacob's eyes turn red as lava and Matthew's as blue as glacial ice. A new battle between neighbors begins.

MY OWN PERSONAL DEMON

The *thing* is currently in my basement. Down the stairs and to the right are my washer and dryer, my utility sink, a few boxes filled with canned goods and bottles of water, a stocked apartment-sized refrigerator, and my own personal demon. It calls to me constantly. This demon wants to be fed and I must answer or it will never stop. For now, the sound is just a murmur, only bothering me a few times an hour. At this level, I can easily resist.

Knock, knock Christine. It's time to feed me.

I sit at my kitchen table sipping a particularly strong cup of coffee - Double French roast with a little sugar and no cream. The brew helps to calm me, to avoid and delay the demon that won't shut up. I feel like I have pretty good control over the situation. I wake up, do my usual morning routine, and sip some coffee before beginning my day. I hear the demon calling me but I have little trouble ignoring the damn thing in the morning, in fact, no trouble at all.

You can't deny me forever. I'm always here, waiting for you.

Frustration is mounting in me. I'm having a few family members over today around 9 a.m., and I'm already a little worried that someone will hear the demon. I don't usually have company over on a Saturday. I generally spend the day unwinding from the work week, watch a little TV, maybe a movie, but I rarely have company. I just feel uncomfortable around my family sometimes. I feel like they are judging me, my decisions, and my life. I'm growing irritated with myself for even allowing visitors, especially on such short notice, but when my brother Nate called last night, he told me there was something very important he needed to discuss with me and it had to be Saturday. I gave in because I just don't like it when people are mad at me. Now I'm angry I agreed. His wife Angela is coming too. She's nice enough but I can always feel the condescending tone in her voice when she talks to me, as if I am beneath her on the evolutionary chart, even though she is ten years younger than I am.

Hey! Hey! What are you waiting for?

At 8:45 a.m., I hear a growl now every few minutes but the sound is still quiet enough for me to avoid. The frequency of the demon calls are increasing, something that doesn't usually occur until much later in the day but I'm fighting hard to wait. I'm growing more and more agitated by the circumstances. I slam my fists down on the table, sloshing a little coffee from my cup.

"Shut up, shut up, shut up!" I stand from my chair, looking around for a dish towel to wipe up the spilled coffee. "I'm getting pissed off. You can wait until they leave. Then, and only then, will I take care of you. You don't control me!"

I shove my chair away from me with the back of my legs and walk over to the sink. I grab the towel lying over the edge and use it clean up my mess. In disgust, I ball the towel up and toss it toward the sink area. I glare at the basement door while taking deep breaths as I defy the urge to give in.

You throw your little tantrum, but sooner or later you will answer me. I own you bitch.

They're going to be here soon. My mind is swimming with ideas on how I can get past this mess. I know I can make it through, I just need a little time. If the demon can just wait until after they leave, everything will be fine. I'm sure they won't be here long. I promise I will feed the stupid, slave-driving, pain in my ass just as soon as Nate and Angela are gone. For now, I need to keep my composure. I beg you, Christine. Stay calm and relax. If we all stay in the living room, no one will hear the howling.

I look to my watch to see how much time I have. Oh crap. They'll be here any minute. I suddenly feel a rumble in the floor boards beneath my feet.

That's right. Deal with those idiots, but when they're gone, you are mine. I cannot be ignored. You need me. Just admit it. Life would suck without me. I make things interesting. You could leave me behind at any time, but guess what, you don't. Why? Because you can't. I am as much a part of you as you are of me.

I stand with my palms planted on the table, wishing there was some way I could end my torture. I hear the demon grumbling incoherently from below. We have both accepted the fact that it will not be fed right now, no way. My heart saddens a little at the thought of my sheer lack of will power. Why do I let myself be bullied? I really need to get some control over the situation. I'm starting to feel helpless and desperate. I know it's a problem. I just can't seem to walk away. I want to, I really do, but I'm scared.

Scared of what my life will be like without it, scared I won't be able to face it, and most of all, scared of the pain.

I start to cry a little before I hear a knocking. I awake from my thoughts but quickly gather myself. I briskly wipe the tears from my face and eyes as I head to the front door.

Awe, baby gonna cry? Hell, you got me all choked up. I'm getting all damn emotional down here. Well, snap out of it! The clock is moving. Tick tock, tick tock. Your time is running out, stupid. It's just a matter of time and you'll be all mine.

I open the door expecting Nate and Angela but am stunned at what I see. Standing behind them is my best friend Maggie, who I work with at the hotel, and my baby sister Kat. I don't know what to make of all this. I know it's not my birthday or anything, so something fishy is going on. I give Nate a stare of frustration and wonder for a few seconds. He finally speaks after a deep breath.

"Hello, Christine. We ... uh ... have something we would all like to talk to you about." Nate pauses a moment. "Can we come in?"

"What the hell are all of you doing here? You didn't tell me they were coming too." I let my disgust for the situation roll off my tongue as I step aside to let everyone in. As each person passes me by, only Nate makes eye contact. The rest of them barely look at me, each with their heads down in shame. They should be ashamed. They all know I hate surprises like this. They better have a damn good explanation for the intrusion.

Everyone gathers in the front room. I have seating for six people, so we all fit easily. They leave the lone recliner at the far end for me. I don't immediately go for it. As a host, I am gracious but still ticked off.

"Does anyone want something to drink? I made coffee, if anyone is interested." I look around the room. Everyone is shaking their heads. I guess that's good. I don't want anyone trailing me into the kitchen. They might hear something. I really don't want to have to explain that.

"Christine, please sit down. We have something very important we would like to discuss with you," Maggie chimes in.

I hear the waver in her voice. The look on everyone's faces is sad and full of distress. Did someone I know die? What the hell is going on? I'm really starting to worry now. Why else would all of them show up unannounced like this? I decide to quell my anger for the moment and sit down.

"Christine, this is very hard for all of us to be here," Nate says with extreme sadness written all over his face. I can barely handle the anticipation, so I interrupt.

"Nate, just tell me what is going on. You are really starting to freak me out. What happened?"

"It's nothing like that. We're all just really worried about you, and we all feel the time has come to intervene. We want to help you." Nate looks around at the faces of the others. "We know you have a big problem that you are having trouble dealing with."

"It's going to be ok, Christine. We all care about you and are here to help," my sister Kat adds.

Oh no. How can they possibly know? It's not like I've ever told anyone about my problem. I feel the panic creep into my hands as they start to shake a little. I just don't know what to expect now.

"I don't even know what you guys are talking about. What problem are you referring to exactly?" Temporarily, my mind drifts back to the demon. I hear a tapping on the underside of the floor beneath where we are all sitting.

Hello, hello, hello. No sense hiding me now. They are on to your little charade. Might as well come on down here and let the party begin. How else are you going to deal with these assholes? You need my help, just admit it. Admit it you bitch!

I'm worried. There is no way they didn't hear that. I look to my hands and see they are still shaking. I try to stay calm but my heart is racing. Secretly, I try to look at the faces of each one of my uninvited guests. Troubled and distressed is how they all look. My anger turns to sadness. I realize my lower lip is quivering, which puts me on the verge of tears.

"Well, we think you know the answer to that. We understand you are not fully in control and we want to help," Nate says. He reaches into the inner pocket of his jacket and pulls out a brochure. "We found this place in town that we think may be able to help. They specialize in this sort of thing." Nate hands the brochure to me.

I look at the front cover and immediately a flood of tears escapes my eyes. There is no sense arguing. I have a serious problem. I know it and they know it. I guess the question is now, what are we going to do about it? I look up at Nate and nod my head. "I know." The words are barely understandable through my sobs.

At this point, all of us women are in tears. Kat gets up and comes over to me. She leans down and hugs me as hard as she can without crushing me. I accept the embrace fully. My best friend Maggie joins us, standing next to my chair. She rubs my shoulder to comfort me.

Oh, this is just ridiculous. How dare you let these people tell you what you need. This ... is ... bullshit! Christine! You seriously need to grow a pair. Send these people out and get your ass down here. Now! This is your last chance. If you leave now, there's no going back. Feeeeeeed Meeeeeeee!

Kat separates from me and sits back down. Maggie does the same. I grab a tissue from the box sitting on the coffee table and blow my nose. I grab another one and wipe the moisture from my eyes and cheeks.

"I know, I know. I want help. I really do. I just don't know how to begin, and frankly, I'm scared. I don't know if I can handle it." I hear the words come out and it feels so good to finally acknowledge the truth. I am suddenly lighter and a wave of relief surges through my body. For the first time ever, I finally accept the fact that I have a big problem and I need help. "So what do I do?"

"Well, that is the tricky part," Nat answers. "To have the best chance of escaping the grip of this ... demon, we need to take action immediately. That way you don't have time to talk yourself out of it." Nate looks me straight in the eye with a seriousness I have never seen from him. "The place in that brochure is expecting you. We would like to take you there right now."

"Now? Like, literally right now?" Fear creeps back into me.

"Right now, there is no other way. It's only for twenty eight days and we'll take care of your personal stuff. We have already talked to your boss and told him the situation. He has agreed to let you off work to get the help you need. Everything is taken care of. We just need you to trust us." Nate looks at his wife for confirmation on how he is handling the situation. She nods.

No, no, no, no, nooooooo!

I grab the hair on the top of my head and pull my face down in an effort to drown out the demon voice. I can no longer stand to hear it. I quell my trepidation, if for no other reason than to escape this damn thing, to keep it from controlling me, harassing me, baiting me. I see a way out and I am ready to jump on it.

"Ok. Let's do this. Just get me out of here, right now. I need to leave this house." I thrust from my chair. I see everyone look to each other, probably confused at my quick acceptance of their offer. I just simply cannot stand the hiding and sneaking and shame. I want it to end.

"This is good," Maggie says as she stands up. Everyone else rises as well. "We all love you so much, Christine. You're doing the right thing."

"Whatever. Let's just go. I need to leave this minute." I rush toward the kitchen. I grab my purse from the table and hear the demon scratching on metal. The sound chills my bones, raising the hair on my arms and legs. "Fuck off!" Staring at the basement door, I release a scream that alarms my family. In disgust, I burst from the kitchen and head right past everyone in the living room and straight out the door. I get into the back seat of Nate's car and break down and cry again.

Maggie, Kat, and Angela rush out to join me. Maggie gets in her own car. In Nate's car, Angela gets in the front seat, Kat gets in the back opposite me. We sit and wait in silence. I think everyone understands that there are no more words needed. Nate finally comes out after a few minutes and drives us away from my home.

About a month has passed and I am home again for the first time since my treatment. Everything looks exactly the same. I enter the kitchen and put my purse down on the table. I take a quick look around and then remove my jacket, placing it on the back of a chair. I walk to the sink and something comes to mind. I open the cabinet door beneath the sink and notice three bottles missing. I realize now why Nate was lingering in the house when I first left. He was removing any trace of temptation for me.

There is one more place he may have forgotten to look - the basement. With hesitation in my steps and my hands, I open the basement door and slowly step down the stairs to face my demon. I think I hear something and pause about halfway down. I listen intently, but nothing. When I reach the bottom, I see my apartment-sized fridge. I find myself unable to move for a full three minutes. I just stare at the brown face of the appliance, contemplating my life and all the hard work I did to get myself clean. Finally, my resolve builds up enough, so I reach out and grab the handle. I gradually draw it open and then gaze at the empty white space inside. My brother must have removed the case of beer that was there, as well as the three bottles of whiskey from under the kitchen sink.

Relief sweeps over my body and I smile. My demon is gone and dead. My new life, free of that torturous beast, can now begin.

THE STING OF FEAR

I've never really cared for insects. They scurry, most are too fast to feel like I have any sort of handle on their presence, and some sting or bite, often passing on diseases or poisoning their unfortunate victims.

Spiders, wasps, hornets, bees, and mosquitoes, in particular, can all burn in hell as far as I am concerned. People wonder why I so feverishly avoid and degrade these creatures with such hostility, and the answer is truthfully, I don't know. I've only been stung once and that was when I was young, probably seven or eight years old. I've been bitten by spiders a few times over the years, but no black widows or brown recluses to report. Of course, if a person likes to spend any time outside, the inevitable mosquito bite on the back of the leg is sure to come, but similarly, no West Nile Virus to account for.

So again, why all the animosity for the creepy-crawlers and ear-buzzers of the world? How can I be so terrified of even the slightest chance encounter with one of these sting demons that I often carry around a badminton racquet at home for protection when I am outside? The answer is still, I don't know.

I can speculate but any ideas I conjure are just theories based on nothing. As a very analytical person, I can see no logical reason for the fear, the panic induced stomping, the girlish screams, or the shallow breathing that arises from the mere thought of just sitting outside on a blistering summer day. My first guess has always been that I was attacked in a past-life and maybe killed by a swarm of bees or hornets. The unexpected and terrifying nature of such an event would shudder the core of most people and it seems as good a reason as any.

I imagine seeing my ten year old self, even though I know it wouldn't be this me in a past life, but it's the only one I can easily muster. I was walking through a grove of trees on a hot summer day, thankful for the shade and the much needed break from the midday sun. I took pleasure in the fresh scent of trees and grasses in full bloom despite the air being thick with humidity.

As I approached a very old, white oak tree with moss covering the bottom three feet, I swatted near my right ear as a buzzing passed back to front. I glanced about to see if the culprit was still around, and after a few seconds, I detected movement on the floor of the forest directly to the left of the giant oak I was so admiring. The bee landed on a small mound of dirt that rested behind a large section of tangled roots from the tree. I inched closer to get a look at what piqued the curiosity of the insect when I spotted another bee coming from a small hole in the ground. My first instinct was to run, but I ignored my impulse and stood staring at the hole, completely fascinated by the swell of bees as one after another streamed outward.

The allure quickly turned into paralyzing fear when I finally caught on to the fact I had stumbled too close and the alarm bells had been sounded. Hundreds of bees circled, attempting to scare me away from their nest. Had I slowly walked away with no panic in my actions, I likely would have made it away unscathed, but like most people in that situation, I freaked out, and my once frozen legs finally became mobile as a series of rhythmic howls escaped my lips. I turned and ran back out of the grove from the same direction I had entered, and the bees followed. With strange, primal noises coming out of my mouth and the sheer terror they could probably sense from every pore in my body, the bees became panicked themselves and they would no longer be satisfied with me simply leaving the area around their home. They had collectively decided that I must be taken out, so no matter how far I ran, they followed.

I threw my arms in the air, waving them about in a mostly failed effort to keep them away from my face. I inhaled and exhaled erratically with no attempt to stay composed. After about one hundred yards I suddenly stopped, maybe to evaluate the situation, maybe just because I was out of breath, but either way, the decision turned out to be the biggest mistake of my life.

One by one, the bees landed on my body, both on my exposed skin and on my clothing, each releasing its pointed fury on me. The stings that broke the skin were each met by a swat or a twist of my torso, all of which were too late to make any difference. Within thirty seconds, the intense pain brought me to my knees. My left eye was already so swollen I couldn't see, and the other one was well on its way. At that point, what little strength I had left in my legs disappeared, flooring me. I writhed around on the ground like I was on fire, rolling once or twice in one direction, only to bolt back the other way, hoping to stop the torture.

One mile from my childhood home in Illinois, in an open grassy area about a hundred feet from the freeway, I was on the ground twitching and spastic with hundreds of red welts, some swelling up to the size of golf balls. My breathing slowed until there were no visible signs I was alive. Finally, my upper body lunged forward about a foot up, violently gasping for one last bit of air before slamming back down to the ground, lifeless.

A few stray bees still crawled around, likely dying, while others buzzed about. Most had already made their way back to the hive, sure that the threat had been eliminated. Their defenses left my body virtually unrecognizable. I doubt my own mother could have identified the body. To top it off, I hadn't told anyone where I was going. No one knew where I was except the bees. No one heard my screams. No one would find my body for three days.

Needless to say, I've thought long and hard about the situation. I constantly rattle positive thoughts in my brain while sitting outside. The usual suspects of reason always come to mind - if you don't bother them they won't bother you, they are more afraid of you than you are of them, blah, blah, blah. I also practice meditative techniques. I close my eyes, breathe in slowly and deeply through my nose, and hold the air until I finally need to exhale. I control my diaphragm using my lower abdomen to push out the air in a steady and calm manner. Once, twice, three times I breathe in and out until I bring myself to a near Zen like state, where nothing big or small could bother me, let alone a rather innocuous insect with no intent to do me any harm.

With my eyes still closed, I inhale deeply one last time, and as I release the air from my lungs, I leisurely open my eyes and stare over the front rail of my porch, totally relaxed.

On one occasion, while sitting outside and feeling pretty confident that my anxiety was in check, I bravely attempted to place my badminton racquet on the table in front of me, ready to give up its questionable protection. Just before the racquet hit the table, a flash of black and yellow zipped past my face, buzzing satanically, snapping me from my trance. In my panicked state, I instinctively drew the racquet toward my face, thwacking the metal edge right into the bridge of my nose. I angrily propelled the racquet away as I yelled and cursed my own stupidity.

I brought a finger to my nose to rub my moustache area, and then quickly pulled my hand away to check for signs of blood. After three attempts, I was grateful to realize I had not broken the skin or forced a nosebleed. It did hurt like a son of a bitch though. I was sure it would swell up nice and big if I didn't get some ice on it, so in I went, having completely forgotten about the original cause of the incident. That was a case of selective memory to be sure.

Well, as you can see, this is not going to be a love story, but more likely a tragedy, mixed with a bit of serendipity, as you will soon see. My imagined past-life experience with bees and my current reality were going to collide, and definitely not in the way one might expect. What happened to me in the summer of 2010 was a surprise, to say the least. This tale doesn't even reside on the outskirts of what a reasonable person might think possible, especially considering my tenuous relationship with the stingers and biters of nature. And so now, my real story begins.

Driving on the back roads of Illinois is about as boring as it gets, even in the summer when everything is growing and green. The corn, the soybeans, and the old farm houses start to blur together into an endless gallery of tiresome sofa-sized paintings. As each framed piece of artwork whizzed by, each one grew more and more indistinguishable.

On an early August day, I made my way home from visiting my mother, who lived three rural towns over, about fifty minutes away. There was nothing particularly interesting about my visit or about the day in general. Of course, when things are at their most mundane, life pokes its head around the corner and hands you a jack-in-a-box, and you mindlessly turn the lever, lulled to sleep by that familiar song. I have always found it amazing how suddenly and unexpectedly life can change. What started out to be just another ordinary day turned out to be simultaneously the most interesting and difficult day I would ever experience for the rest of my life.

The deer caught me completely by surprise. I knew the roads well enough to let my full attention lapse sometimes, but in Illinois, that can lead to dangerous consequences. As I turned a moderately sharp corner, not so much so that I needed to slow down but almost blind from the large, hilled section directly after it, my SUV collided violently with a mature doe. She wasn't terribly large, but at that speed and with no time to even touch the brakes before impact, the doe ripped open like a can of sardines and was thrown at least a hundred feet down the road. My SUV suffered a similar fate, at least in the sense that it would never run again.

Within two seconds of contact, my steering wheel airbag exploded into my face, releasing a poof of white powder into the air. The force broke my sunglasses in half, which subsequently gashed my face from the middle of my nose, down and across my right cheek, just shy of the bottom of my ear lobe. Startled, I slammed on the brakes, doubling the percussion of the accident. Steering madly to the left in a delayed attempt to avoid the animal, my actions forced the rear of the vehicle to swing around, putting me perpendicular to the road. Once there, the momentum stopped from the tires grabbing the pavement and the vehicle was propelled like a clunky barrel rolling down the road, angled slightly toward a massive ravine just off the right hand side. After a few complete revolutions, the SUV tumbled down the embankment, still rolling and tossing me around with it until finally settling upside down about fifty feet from an overpass bridge that carried the road over a small creek.

With no rain for two weeks, the creek itself was only about six inches deep and my inverted SUV came to rest just a foot from the water. The front end was almost completely crushed and smoke billowed from what was left of the engine and the front end. The cage of the vehicle was reduced to about one third of its original size, with the wheels bent and pointed in all directions. Oddly enough, the driver's side front tire spun rather lopsided and dysfunctional for a few minutes after the crash, while the others were no longer capable. None of the windows remained, including the windshield, which had popped off in one big, spider web like piece, landing in a ditch after the first full roll.

I was in no better shape. My face was bleeding profusely but looked worse than it actually was, and I had a severe concussion and whiplash from my head being slammed backwards against the head rest. My right ankle was broken from the contact it made with the center console as the SUV rolled into the ravine. My entire left side suffered severe bruising but nothing was broken, and of course, I was uncomfortably upside down, secured by my seatbelt. Good times.

The effects of the crash left me muddled, and within moments of the vehicle coming to rest, unconscious as well. I had no idea the smoke coming from the front of my mangled SUV was now a small fire and I was half covered in gasoline and other engine fluids. Now, any reasonable reader might ask, what does any of this have to do with bees, past lives, and illogical fear? That, my friend, is coming soon, so please bear with me.

I awoke later in the day with the sun still out, probably close to five o'clock in the evening. To my surprise, I was no longer in my SUV. In fact, I was lying on the ground next to a tree about a half-mile from the crash site. I was a little confused about the entire incident, and even more so about my current circumstances. I could barely recall the impact, or flipping and rolling the vehicle, but I did remember the sound of my driver's side door being pried open. Perhaps firefighters had used the Jaws of Life to rescue me from what could have been my steel and fiberglass coffin.

Nope. A local farmer had noticed my SUV in the ravine whilst surveying the edges of his property. He had climbed down the embankment, checked my pulse to make sure I was still alive, and when he found that I was, he was able to muscle my car door open with his bare hands. At six foot, four inches tall and about two hundred sixty-five pounds, it was no surprise he could manage such a feat.

He released my seatbelt but caught me as I fell, then lifted me out of the car and dropped me hard to the ground about twenty feet away. He proceeded to climb back up the embankment to where his work truck was located, and then backed it up to the edge of the ravine. On the rear of the truck was a tow cable apparatus. I assumed it was for pulling tractors and other things from the mud when they got stuck. He grabbed the large metal hook and climbed back down the hill, pulling the steel cable along with him. When he reached my SUV, he attached the hook somewhere on what was left of the front end, and up he went to engage the winch. The motor whirred as it dragged the wreckage through the shallow creek and up the side of the ravine. Ultimately, it ended up in one of his very large outbuildings, about a half-mile back from the road.

Why would a local farmer go to all this trouble and not just have called 9-1-1? Why would he take it upon himself to rescue me only to throw me hastily to the ground and then tow my vehicle, not just out of the ravine, but all the way back to one of his barns? I would find out soon enough.

I was still drifting in and out, my memory scrambled. I was trying desperately to focus when I heard the crunch of someone walking nearby. After hiding my SUV, the farmer arrived back at the spot he left me. He grabbed me by the ankle, but not the broken one, hallelujah, or the damage could have been much worse. He dragged me away from the creek bed until we got to an area where the land flattened out and there was a little makeshift cabin, probably used for hunting. The farmer released my leg near a large tree that stood about twenty feet from the cabin, and I was left there while the farmer went inside to make his preparations. I got dizzy, closed my eyes, and passed out again.

About five minutes later, I regained consciousness, totally confused and a little scared, wondering what the hell had just happened. I barely remembered the accident, and I could only recall flashes of the events during the towing and dragging. As far as I was concerned, this guy had helped me and the cavalry was on the way. Boy was I wrong. I had no clue that our seemingly generous and altruistic farmer had more sinister things in mind for me.

While on the ground attempting to assess my situation, some of the feeling in my body returned. The first thing I noticed was a strange, overpowering smell, but that quickly passed as the throbbing of my monstrous headache took hold. To top that, when I placed my right hand on the ground and started to pull my knees to my chest to prop myself up, I received what can only be described as a jolt of electricity that shot from my right foot straight up through my entire leg. I screamed in anguish as I grabbed my swelling ankle that had grown to the size of a grapefruit. I could only assume it was broken because pain that bad never came from just a sprain.

As I tried to internalize the pain, I glanced around, hoping to see some signs of the accident that set this adventure in motion. Instead, I saw the small hunting cabin and a number of thoughts ran through my mind. Who is this guy that brought me here? Did he call for help? Why the hell did he bring me all the way out here? I was shaken from my thoughts by a rustling noise in the cabin.

"Hello? Is anybody there?" I waited, listening for a response, anxious and desperate for an answer. "I'm pretty badly hurt, and I think I need an ambulance." I paused for about five seconds. "Hello?" Again, I tilted my head toward the cabin and listened carefully.

Suddenly, the cabin door flew open and slammed against the front wall, scaring the crap out of me. Through the doorway exited a very large and intimidating man, dressed like the quintessential Illinois farmer - blue jean overalls, a white, crew-cut short sleeve shirt, and a green baseball cap with a white front. He had an ominous looking shovel in his left hand that rested upright against his shoulder. I swore I heard a banjo playing.

"Well, well. Look who finally woke up. That's too bad ... for you anyhow. This would have been much easier for ya had ya stayed out."

The farmer walked toward me and when he got close enough, he pulled the shovel off his shoulder and held the metal end up like a baseball bat, ready to swing.

"I don't know what is going on here, but I am seriously injured." Before I could finish my thought, the farmer took two steps to get behind me and unleashed the shovel into the back of my head, sending my torso violently forward. In agony, I fell backwards a few seconds later, landing flat on the ground, hard. How I remained conscious from that blow, especially considering I already had a concussion, is still a mystery to this day. The blow, however, did temporarily rob the air from my lungs.

Stunned, I decided to keep my eyes closed and not move a muscle, hoping my assailant would believe I was out cold. It appeared to work. About a minute later, the farmer grabbed my bad ankle and pulled me in the direction of the cabin. I howled in pain and nearly blacked out. Luckily, I stayed conscious, and without time to weigh the possibilities, I concluded it was time to fight. I twisted away from my kidnapper and slipped right out of his hand, landing on my stomach. I then lifted myself onto my hands and knees and began crawling away.

"Boy! Git your ass back here! I ain't through with you yet. Where the fuck you gonna crawl to anyway?"

He reached down again, snatched me by the good ankle this time, and pulled twice as hard. En route, I heard a buzzing sound around my head. Out of the corner of my swollen eye, I saw an old, jagged tree stump to my right. Bees entered and exited small holes in the side, and some from the top. Normally, my phobia of all things creepy-crawly would have forced me to panic and flee, but obviously, I had bigger fish to fry, and I couldn't exactly run away, even if I wanted to.

A plan came to mind and against my better judgment, I once again tried to escape the farmer's grasp by twisting wildly in the direction of the stump. As I did, I clawed at its base and the ground around it. Fortunately, the adrenaline took care of my pain. At first, the farmer barely fought back, temporarily releasing his grip, only to grab my pant leg instead, but this allowed me to get my face within a foot of the hive. Without being completely sure what I hoped to accomplish, I continued digging rampantly before finally just pounding the ground like a misfit two-year old throwing a tantrum. On red alert, hundreds and hundreds of bees exited the hive, flying furiously in defense of their home. The area around us darkened and trembled. Within seconds we were surrounded, but with my broken ankle, I had no chance of getting away. The farmer, on the other hand, had one good option - Get in the cabin.

He let go of my pants and frantically swung his arms in the air as he stumbled toward shelter. He fought hard against our mutual enemy. As he did, I returned to my hands and knees, hoping I could get some distance between me, the hive, and the farmer. Much to my delight, only a few bees hovered around me as I made my getaway. Oddly, none of them actually landed on me. They danced around in the air and buzzed by my head, warning me to get away, and I did my best to comply.

Finally, I stopped and shifted my weight around to my backside so I could get a look back at the cabin. The door was still wide open but on the ground I saw the farmer, his arms twitching and foam coming from his mouth in a gurgling sound. The bees had concentrated their attack on him, bringing that poor bastard to the ground in anaphylactic shock. Once down, he lasted only a couple of minutes before his heart stopped. I, however, suffered not one bee sting, even though I was the one who had disturbed the hive to begin with.

Auspiciously, I found my cell phone in my pocket and was able to call for help. How I didn't realize the phone was there earlier was beyond me but I was sure glad it was. The entire gamut of rescue personnel arrived within twenty minutes using the signal from my phone to track my location. I told the authorities everything I could remember. Upon further inspection, they found three full human skeletons and a couple of partial ones in and around the cabin. In fact, this farmer had a nasty little secret of snatching strangers and doing god knows what to them. By ignoring my own fears in a life or death situation, I may have actually saved a few people from a similar fate to those unfortunate victims before me. Now we'll never know, and I'm happy about that.

I was also told the gasoline and engine fluids on my body saved my life that day. The bees didn't want to come near me smelling the way I did. It somehow offended them. *I* offended them? Apparently, I repulsed them the way they once repulsed me. However, from that day forward, I would no longer hate and fear the buzzing, creeping, crawling, stinging, and biting insects of the Earth. I revered them. I was grateful for them. I would thank them every day for the rest of my life.

AUTHOR'S NOTES

Neither Snow, Nor Rain, Nor Zombie Infection

My wife and I were out shopping one day, and I had zombies on the brain. We were at shopping center that still had six or seven businesses, but the large anchor store had closed a few years before then, making that part seem abandoned. A mail truck drove by, having just delivered mail to the still open businesses in the strip mall, and with my mind on zombies from having just watched a movie about them; I wondered if zombies, while they were in the process of turning, would still do their jobs, i.e. a mailman zombie. I brought up the idea with my wife and we laughed about the prospect of seeing a mail carrier walking down the street, dragging a leg, and carrying a bag full of letters. Silly. I thought about writing it as a television show where everybody was a zombie, but otherwise, they lived life like they always had. When I began writing other short stories and realized I wanted to put together a collection, I came up with Hank and ran with it. I thought it would be interesting to write a zombie story where the protagonist was the zombie instead of someone battling the zombies. It's a bittersweet story and my wife's favorite from the collection.

The Eyes

I actually wrote part of this story in the late nineties. I originally intended the concept to become a full novel but as I prepared this collection, I re-read it and thought it might make a great short story. The protagonist is basically caught in a mental loop and the reader doesn't really know why, and neither does he. When I read it, I have more questions than answers, and that is exactly what I had hoped to accomplish. I still have no idea what is happening to this guy, you can decide for yourself.

Failure Rate: 100%

I'm a fan of Isaac Asimov but I have always thought the Laws of Robotics were flawed to some degree. No matter how much thought we put into protecting ourselves, we cannot account for everything. There are bound to be some issues, so I thought up a crazy idea about a robot malfunctioning and keeping its master prisoner because it could not understand that it's ok for humans to make mistakes. And since we humans often do things that put our lives in danger, and we do these things by choice, I could imagine an android having trouble dealing with that. I love technology though, and I am anxious to see where it takes us in my lifetime.

This Year's Featured Guests

90% of this story came to me as a dream. Originally, it took place on the streets of New Orleans and not on a major compound. As I outlined and started writing the story, I couldn't easily work out some of the logistics with everything taking place in the middle of a major city, so I shifted the setting. I think it worked out much better and it became much easier for me to keep it 'real'. I told my wife about the dream right after it happened, and that I thought it would be an awesome book. She agreed. It would be another seven or eight years before I would actually write it, but I'm so glad I finally did. I quickly realized there was not enough there to write an entire book from the story, so it became the perfect thing to do for this collection. I hope every time you enter a contest to win a trip, you think long and hard about the consequences.

Don't Mess with the Babysitter

Originally, this story was much darker, and quite violent. In fact, the title was *Don't Fuck with the Babysitter*, but as I read over the notes and the first few pages, it became clear to me that the story was too light-hearted and funny to have such heavy overtones, so I changed it a little. For the most part, the story is the same, just not as edgy. I know it can be difficult to read with the first-person language of Brandy dominating, but I could not tell the story with the same impact unless I remained true to the protagonist's voice, literally. Not everyone will enjoy it, or get it, but if you can buy into the concept, I think you will like it.

They Smell the Dead

There is a scene in the movie *Ghost* with Patrick Swayze and Demi Moore where these black, ghostly demons take the bad guy away after he dies. This story is my homage to that scene, except the little demons are vultures. Whenever there is something dead, on or near the road, I see the vultures circling overhead, so if there is a living creature that might be hanging around right before we die, the vulture would be it. For the first time in my life, I actually witnessed a kettle of vultures in a field about two weeks before I wrote this note. I was fascinated. I counted twenty-two of them in the field, but on the way back by after grocery shopping, I realized there were many more of them in the trees that lined the back of the field. It was one of the coolest things I have ever seen. The weird thing too was that they weren't actually all standing in one big group, but rather they were broken up into smaller groups of five or six, spread out across the field and trees. It reminded me of every gathering of people I have ever been to. We often separate into little cliques when in large groups, and apparently vultures do too.

A Neighborly Scourge

As the treasurer of my homeowner's association, I see and hear the best and worst of being part of a neighborhood. I know we all wish that sometimes we could launch a fireball at some house, not really wanting to hurt anyone, maybe just to send a message, but we do our best to be civil. I must have just watched one of the Harry Potter movies or something, but when the idea popped into my head about two neighbors fighting over a tree branch, and they happened to be wizards, I had to develop a story around the idea. It's as simple as that.

My Own Personal Demon

If you hadn't figured it out, this story is an allegory for someone dealing with addiction. I came up with the idea probably ten years ago but never had the guts to write the story. It can be an emotional read; it certainly was an emotional write. The woman goes through the five stages of grief as she gets close to killing her demon. I hope that anyone who can relate to this tale sees it as a story of hope and not despair. Addiction is one big SOB, but there is hope and people do succeed, so don't ever give up. Be honest, get help, and take your life back from that fucking demon.

RICHARD A. POWELL II

The Sting of Fear

I am scared shitless of wasps and bees and such. I have been asked if this tale is autobiographical, but aside from the fear, it is complete fiction. Well ... I do occasionally carry a badminton racket around when I am outside in the heat of summer, but other than that, the story is a tall-tale. I wrote the story in one sitting and it became my inspiration for the entire short story collection. For the record, I also happen to be afraid of becoming a hoarder, carnies, rabid raccoons, the Twilight movies, drowning, and speaking in front of crowds. Is anything I've written here true? Do you have to ask? The Twilight movies? That's some scary shit.

ABOUT THE AUTHOR

Richard A. Powell II currently lives with his wife Amy in Bloomington, Illinois, where he enjoys DIY projects, disc golf, technology, playing video games, and reading and writing (obviously). He is also a self-professed nerd/geek, but no, he will not fix your computer, unless you ask really, really nicely and offer him perfectly cooked bacon.

www.richardapowellii.com
richard.powell74@gmail.com

RICHARD A. POWELL II